"Neither the
is as fixed and certain as people
would like to think," Thomas said.

"But some futures are worse than others, and I mean to stop the worst one from being the one that sticks."

"That's a mighty big job."

Thomas shrugged a little. "Where I am now, I don't have much else to occupy my mind."

"How do you propose to go about it?"

"By talking to the man who has the power to act."

"Meaning me, I suppose."

"No other," Thomas agreed. "I'll come back here someday, and when that day comes around, you'll need to do what I tell you."

"What happens," said the president, "if I don't?"

"Ask Mrs. Lincoln," said Thomas. "She already knows."

By Debra Doyle and James D. Macdonald

LINCOLN'S SWORD
LAND OF MIST AND SNOW

LINCOLN'S SWORD

DEBRA DOYLE
AND JAMES D. MACDONALD

An Imprint of HarperCollins*Publishers*

EOS
An Imprint of HarperCollins*Publishers*
10 East 53rd Street
New York, New York 10022–5299

Copyright © 2010 by Debra Doyle and James D. Macdonald
Cover art by Steve Stone
ISBN 978–0–06–081927–9
www.eosbooks.com

First Eos paperback printing: August 2010

This book is for Kathryn Salter Jackson,
who's come to our rescue more
than once when things got crazy.
Thanks, Kate, for everything.

Acknowledgments

We would like to thank Verlaine Daeron and Marc Ounis, of Le Rendez-Vous Bakery in Colebrook, New Hampshire, for letting us hold down a table to work on while finalizing the manuscript of this novel, for nothing more than the price of some excellent coffee and pastries. We would also like to thank our agent, Russ Galen, and our editors, Diana Gill and Will Hinton, for their great and extreme patience and support.

"I have not allowed myself, Sir, to look beyond the Union, to see what might lie hidden in the dark recess behind. I have not coolly weighed the chances of preserving liberty when the bonds that unite us together shall be broken asunder. I have not accustomed myself to hang over the precipice of disunion, to see whether, with my short sight, I can fathom the depth of the abyss below; nor could I regard him as a safe counsellor in the affairs of this government, whose thoughts should be mainly bent on considering, not how the Union may be best preserved, but how tolerable might be the condition of the people when it should be broken up and destroyed. While the Union lasts, we have high, exciting, gratifying prospects spread out before us and our children. Beyond that I seek not to penetrate the veil. God grant that in my day, at least, that curtain may not rise! God grant that on my vision never may be opened what lies behind! When my eyes shall be turned to behold for the last time the sun in heaven, may I not see him shining on the broken and dishonored fragments of a once glorious Union; on States dissevered, discordant, belligerent; on a land rent with civil feuds, or drenched, it may be, in fraternal blood! Let their last feeble and lingering glance rather behold the gorgeous ensign of the republic, now known and honored throughout the earth, still full high advanced, its arms and trophies streaming in their original lustre, not a stripe erased or polluted, not a single star obscured, bearing for its motto, no such miserable interrogatory as "What is all this worth?" nor those other words of delusion and folly, "Liberty first and Union afterwards"; but everywhere, spread all over in characters of living light, blazing on all its ample folds, as they float over the sea and over the land, and in every wind under the whole heavens, that other sentiment, dear to every true American heart,—Liberty *and* Union, now and for ever, one and inseparable!"

—DANIEL WEBSTER, 1830, *Second Reply to Hayne*

1916

Lee's Summit, Missouri

THOMAS was an old man now, and he hadn't gone shifting himself between one time and another for quite a few years, not since he'd gotten out of prison and left Minnesota for good. The world beyond the prison walls had too many people in it, and too much noise; and he thought that he had already done everything a man could do to finish the job that he'd been given. There wasn't anyone left alive who could say different, that much was sure.

He'd never met another man who possessed his gifts in every particular. Maybe there were a few who had the possibility of it, but if he were still the betting man that he had been in his youth, he would have wagered good money that no one else had been given—as he had been given, although much against his will—the extremes of quiet and seclusion that were needed to develop them.

But in this Year of Our Lord 1916, every day the papers brought bad news of the war that was raging in Europe—stories of British troops retreating from Turkey, of zeppelins attacking Paris from the air, of bloody battles on the ground in Belgium and France. Then there were the other stories that the newspapers didn't tell, the stories that passed from one cunning-man or wise-woman to another like a river of hidden knowledge running underground. A woman in Paris, they said, had called up one of the great salamanders and imprisoned it inside a brass shell, and a man in the Ruhr Valley had learned the master-word that compelled the dark spirits of the mountains to craft for him monstrous guns of adamant metal; and it was only chance that had put them on opposite sides of the war and kept them from joining together to make a weapon more terrible than anyone had yet seen. And there were other stories like that, or worse, as if Europe were tearing itself to pieces and taking the rest of the world along with it.

Everything he'd done before, he'd done in the name of preventing a dreadful future that he could only dimly perceive—the clear sight had always been someone else's gift, not his—and he had trouble believing that what he saw happening now was the result of success and not of failure. He was oppressed by the fear that all the work he'd done had still not been enough, or that he had, in spite of himself, done wrong, causing by his efforts all of the things that he had tried to prevent.

He spent a great deal of time sleeping these days. It came, he supposed, from having lived so much longer than he'd ever expected to. By most men's reckoning, he ought to have gone down bloody and bullet-ridden years ago—he'd certainly endured gunfire enough for it—instead of being well on the way to dying peace-fully in his own bed. And in Missouri, no less, which was more luck than he probably deserved.

The benefit of sleeping so much in his old age was that nobody was ever surprised to see him stretched out on his bed in the afternoon, with his eyes closed and his breathing deep and steady. They'd tiptoe away, saying "Don't disturb the poor old gentleman; he needs his rest," and they wouldn't come back and bother him until suppertime. That left plenty of room for a man like him to go traveling.

It was a skill hard learned. The boy who had first been shown the way had not followed it—he'd had too many other things calling to him, kin and country and desperate deeds, and a wild life outside the law. Not until the wild days ended and the law had its grip on him did he take the time to practice what he had been taught. Time, after all, was the one thing a prisoner had in abundance, and he had made full use of the time he'd been given.

When he'd taken up the work again in these latter days, he'd tried going forward, further into 1916 and beyond, into the possible futures, good and bad, that he saw fanning out from the present. He couldn't. He could see them, like faded photographs on the other side of a sheet of thick glass, but that was the outer limit of his agency. He could not move into those futures, or affect them, by which he understood that his time on earth remaining was short. He had known for a long time that he couldn't shift forward beyond the end of his physical life in this, his native plane. If there was any part of his work that he had neglected or left undone, he would have to finish it now.

He rose from his bed and stepped away from his sleeping body. The man who lay there, breathing steadily and deeply, did not look as he remembered himself looking when he rode with Quantrill into Lawrence, or into Northfield with Frank and the boys. This other man looked old and worn down and tired, even in his sleep, with a furrowed face and close-cropped hair gone grey.

I wasn't so bad-looking once, he thought. *Don't think I could charm the ladies like I used to, not anymore.*

He had work to do, and only a little while left to do it in. Moving away from the here and the now, he let himself wander through past years with no specific destination in mind, never staying for too long in one time or place. To an outside observer in any of those places, he might have seemed to flicker into existence and back out again, if indeed his presence had been noted at all. But there was nothing anywhere that seemed likely to help him, at least not until he heard the voice speaking to him from somewhere deep in the many-layered past.

"Come here and see me. I'm waiting to talk with you."

1791

Northwest Territory,
Banks of the Wabash

THE campfires of the regulars and militiamen made scattered patches of yellow-orange across the dark ground, and the waters of the Wabash River gave back the pattern of lights in the blackness like a sullen mirror. The night air was cold, with the sodden heaviness of impending snow, and thick clouds covered the moon and the stars.

Major-General Richard Butler paused for a moment outside his commander's tent, where the light from a single lantern shone through the stretched linen, silhouetting the camp bed and the table and the backless chair within. Then he lifted the tent flap and went inside.

The interior of the tent was scarcely warmer than the exterior. The chair was empty, although the maps and papers on the table, weighted down by an inkwell and a pair of spectacles, suggested that it had been occupied not too long before. General Arthur St. Clair lay on the cot, covered by a woollen blanket. He raised himself up on one elbow as Butler entered.

"General Butler," he said. There was a querulous

note in his voice that Butler did not like. "Sit down. It makes my neck ache to look up at you."

"Thank you, sir." Butler sat down in the camp chair—carefully; he was a big man, both in inches and in the weight of flesh and bone—and regarded the army's commander.

General St. Clair suffered from gout and felt the cold keenly. Butler had thought from the beginning of this campaign that it had been a cruel trick to give the work of securing the Northwest Territory of the new republic to a man of St. Clair's years, and one whose long service to his country deserved better. The general should have been resting at home in a warm dressing gown by his own hearth, rather than enduring privation and foul weather; and the army should have had a leader who wasn't half crippled by pain, and made ill-tempered by it as well.

"Well," demanded St. Clair. "What is it you've come here to say?"

Butler didn't want to raise the subject of the scouts, not with St. Clair in this mood, but duty demanded that he try. "Major Dark believes that the Shawnee and the Miami are out in force, and the Lenape also."

"He believes that, does he? And where comes he by this intelligence?"

"From the scouts, he says."

"The scouts." St. Clair gave a snort. "Militiamen, the lot of them, and afraid of their own shadows. Not a week in the woods among them."

Butler had to admit that St. Clair had a point. The frontier militia were untrained and unreliable, and had always shown a tendency to break under fire and to take leave of the army whenever it pleased them to do so. He wasn't even certain if it was fair to call it desertion when one of the parties involved seemed to have no concept of the military discipline that they flouted with such regularity.

On the other hand—"They know this part of the country better than we do, and most of them have been living close by the savages since they were first able to draw breath."

"Too damned close, some of them," said St. Clair. "There's that renegade—what's his name—with the Lenape—"

"Simon Girty," said Butler heavily. "Our scouts despise him."

"Still. It's indicative. They're not a trustworthy people."

"I think we should put the pickets out farther, just in case," Butler said.

"No. I want them close in. Otherwise they'll hear an owl hoot and think that it's the whole Shawnee nation."

"Yes. But if it isn't an owl, we'll be thankful for the warning later."

"They're militia," St. Clair said. "Put them too far out, and they'll be no good regardless of what happens—they'll bolt at the first sign of trouble, and spread panic among the others."

Butler suppressed a sigh. St. Clair had a certain amount of reason on his side. Panic acted like a contagion on untried troops, and frightened men could turn surprise into rout with appalling speed. Weighing that possibility against the possibility of surprise . . . *We are different men; he sees the scales tilted one way, and I another. But he commands the army, and I do not. We*

are not the antique Romans, to divide the command evenly
between two consuls, each one countermanding the other on
alternate days until nothing is accomplished.

"I'll give the word to keep the pickets in close," he
said. "Do you still intend that the army march again
in the morning?"

St. Clair nodded. "Tell the officers, be ready to strike
the tents after the men have had their breakfast."

"I will," he said. "Is there anything more you need
done?"

"No."

St. Clair lay back on his pillow. Once again, Butler
was struck by his pallor. "Put out the lantern when
you go. I had thought to rise up after I had rested for
a while, and do more work, but I find that I am tired
and need to sleep."

Butler did as he was told, and left the tent behind
him in darkness. The exchange with St. Clair had left
him irritable and morose, as so many of his conversa-
tions with the army's commander did. He felt a surge
of sudden nostalgia for the days of the revolution,
when he had been a younger and a lighter man, with
a commander he would have happily died for, and a
true victory in sight at the end of it.

And I was the one chosen to take Cornwallis's sword, for
the honor of it all.

Whatever else has changed, I still have those. My honor,
and the sword.

He made his way through the camp, seeing to the
placement of the pickets and making arrangements
for the morning meal, before turning toward the tent
that he shared with his brothers. Thomas and Edward
were both there ahead of him. Edward was a sleeping
lump wrapped in a blanket and an army cape, while

Thomas sat outside by the embers of their dying fire, drinking liquor from a metal flask.

"How went the matter of Major Dark and his scouts?" Thomas asked.

"As well as I expected," Butler said. "Which is to say, badly. St. Clair puts no faith in the militia, or any of its works."

Thomas offered him the flask. "Have a sip of consolation. Our commander has a point, you know—the scouts have been seeing Indians where there aren't any for weeks."

"They've been finding Indian sign," Butler said. He took a long swallow from Thomas's flask, which turned out to hold strong Jamaica rum cut with water, and made a noise of pleasure. "I won't ask you where you got this, as far from civilization as we are—"

"I have my ways," Thomas said.

"And I'm damned grateful for them." He handed back the flask. "Maybe we'll go from one side of the Northwest Territory to the other finding Indian sign but no Indians—if the savages don't want to engage with us directly, it's easy enough for them to be someplace where we're not. But."

"Yes. There's always that 'but.' What do you intend to do about it?"

"If I were the commander?" Butler asked. "I'd put out more pickets, post them farther away from camp, and set the artillery where it could support the line."

"You're not the commander," Thomas pointed out.

"I know. Therefore, instead of putting out pickets, I intend to sharpen my sword, then get as much sleep as I can before morning."

The next day dawned grey and clammy, a wet cold that soaked through to the bone. Richard Butler woke early, before the first bugle sounded to rouse the camp. He dressed quickly, buckling on his sword and swinging his campaign cloak onto his shoulders, then prodded first Edward, then Thomas with the toe of his boot.

"Up," he said. "If we start now, we can break our own fast before we have to start turning out the men and making sure that they're fed properly. I don't want them forced to march on empty stomachs in this weather, just because some slug-a-bed officer wanted to keep his feet warm for a few minutes longer."

Edward and Thomas grumbled—neither of them was an early riser by choice—but the habit of obedience to their older brother was strong, and they did his bidding. Gradually, to the sound of drums and bugles, the rest of the camp began stirring to life. A low, patchy mist lay on the ground by the Wabash, and the figures of men loomed up in it and faded back again as the soldiers of St. Clair's army prepared their morning meal and struck their tents. The clouds overhead were a thin grey like the mist; Butler guessed that the sun would burn through them by midday. The warmth and light would come too late to make for a pleasant morning's march, but a late sunshine was still better than no sunshine at all.

"Not a good day for the General's gout," Thomas said—he must have caught Butler's glance upward, and the change of expression on his face. "He'll be in a foul mood by evening, and cursing the scouts for a pack of damned liars."

"What if the scouts are right?" Edward asked. He was younger than Richard or Thomas, still new to campaigning and apt to be apprehensive. At the moment, the tip of his nose and the rims of his ears were reddened by the cold, making him look even younger than his actual years, like a schoolboy attending unwillingly upon the bell. "What if Little Turtle and the Shawnee really are out in force?"

"Then St. Clair will be cursing the scouts for not bringing the word to him sooner," Thomas said. " 'Tis the way of generals."

Butler aimed a mock cuff at his head. "Speak respectfully of your elder brother, you rascal."

"And so I will, just as soon as—" Thomas broke off in mid-sentence and cocked his head, listening. "Did you hear that?"

"No," Butler said. Then, "Wait. Yes."

Edward gazed at them both, wide-eyed. "What is it? I don't hear—"

The wind shifted and the sounds came again, louder this time: the rattle-and-snap of musket fire and a high-pitched ululating yell.

"Indians," said Butler, drawing his sword and starting out toward the infantry lines at a run. "Close upon us."

I was right, he thought as he ran. *We should have put the pickets out farther.*

The men were in grave disarray, militia and regulars alike. The Shawnee had opened fire upon them as they were gathering for breakfast—somebody in the Indian camp, Butler thought, had a good idea of when the army would be at its most vulnerable.

A young lieutenant emerged from the press at Butler's right hand, shouting, "Form line, damn you, form line!" at the infantrymen trying to flee, and slapping at them with the flat of his sword. Butler heard the whine of a musket ball as it passed close by his ear, and a heartbeat later the wet sound of impact as it struck flesh and someone close behind him cried out in pain.

The war whoops of the Shawnee and the Miami and the Lenape rose up on all sides. Musket volleys answered them, but ragged and short, not the disciplined mass of fire that was needed to break irregular troops like Little Turtle's Indian warriors. Where Edward and Thomas were in the press, Butler could not tell; like him, they had sped away at the sound of the alarm, gone to join—and, God willing, to rally—their own men. He saw St. Clair on horseback, briefly through the mist, plumed hat in hand, gesturing with it to wave the infantry forward.

It was a wasted effort; the frightened men paid their general no heed. "Devil take the militia!" swore the young lieutenant. "The bastards understand no order save 'cut and run'!"

"Little good it will do them," said Richard. "Keep the regulars in order, Lieutenant, and we will do what we can."

Arrows flew now, the thrumming of their passage mixed in with the rattle of musketry. Not all the Indians had firearms, but it didn't matter. The head of an arrow could punch through a uniform tunic as easily as a musket ball, and kill a man just as dead. Soon enough, the tomahawks and war clubs would come into play.

The mist and the powder smoke swirled away again for an instant. St. Clair, on a fresh horse—*they've already killed the first one under him,* Butler thought—loomed up briefly and wheeled away again, shouting, "Cowards! Cowards!" to no avail at the fleeing troops.

"God save us, General," said the lieutenant. "This is a rout."

The man's cheeks and forehead were black with gunpowder, and blood ran down the side of his face from a tomahawk's grazing blow. Butler remembered killing the Shawnee that had dealt it, but could not remember how the Indian had come so close.

"The cannons," Butler said, thinking, *Little Turtle is no fool, nor Blue Jacket either. I would not want to place a wager against either one of them knowing what to do with artillery pieces.* "We have to destroy them. Take what regulars you can hold together, sir, and see to it."

"Yes, sir." The man seemed happier for having been given a clear order. Butler heard him shouting at the nearby infantry, then vanishing with them into the smoke and the press of battle.

Good, he thought. *That's taken care of, at least.*

His body hurt; he felt a pain in his side as though someone had hit him with a heavy club . . . somebody probably had; it distressed him that he could not recall the blow . . . and his legs felt weak. He touched his thigh, and felt a stickiness there that he recognized as blood.

"Richard!" It was Edward, hatless and for some reason coatless as well, appearing suddenly out of the smoke and yelling and confusion. "Tom's hurt! I need your help to—" His eyes struck full on Butler for the first time, and his voice cracked.

"Do what you can for Thomas," Butler said. His legs weren't up to supporting him any longer; he sank to the ground, thankful for the way that Edward leaped forward to catch him and help him down. "I'll be staying here, I think."

"Richard—"

"Good-bye, Edward."

"Good-bye," came the choked response. He felt

Edward embrace him briefly and place a kiss of fare-well on his forehead; then his brother was gone.

The lieutenant was back. He'd lost his hat, and blood and dirt befouled the blue cloth and gold trim of his uniform tunic. More blood ran down the length of his sword, from tip almost to hilt.

"We've spiked the guns, sir," he said. "The Indians won't have them."

"Good." Butler found it hard to speak; his lungs didn't seem to want to push out enough air to give volume to his words. "Take the men you have left, and retreat in the best order you can."

"But, General Butler, sir—"

"I'm dying." *Bleeding my life out into the dirt, and if I'm lucky I'll be gone before the Shawnee take their knives and tomahawks to me.* "One thing."

"Sir?"

"My sword." He fumbled at the hilt. His fingers had grown clumsy, and slipped away from the grip. "Take it to my brothers, if either lives. And tell them not to wash the blood of the Butlers clean from the blade."

The lieutenant took the sword and lifted it away. "I will," he said.

"Tell them—stay faithful to the Republic," Butler said. But the lieutenant, and the sword, were already gone.

1834
Baltimore, Maryland

EVERYONE, Mercy Levering's mother had told her when she was just a girl, is born with a gift. Not always a great gift—a light hand with pie crust, or a sure eye for a good horse, or a heart made to be cheerful in adversity—but a gift from God all the same.

Mercy's own gift had been something greater than any of those, but her mother had never seen it. Others had, over the years: the black freedwoman who had cooked for the family when she was six, and who drew strange complicated pictures in the dust of the hearth and spoke to her in the voice of a heathen god; the dressmaker when she was ten, who came from the Pennsylvania Dutch country and talked of hoodoo and hex signs, and passed along a dog-eared copy of *The Long-Lost Friend* that Mercy even then knew better than to let her mother find; the schoolmaster when she was fifteen, who never said a word in class about gifts or the people who had them, but left the key to his locked bookshelf on her desk one afternoon, and looked the other way when she borrowed the old, dark volumes one at a time for over a year.

When she was eleven years old, she laid her slate

on the ground and drew a circle on it with chalk, and marked symbols in the circle at north and south and east and west, and spoke words under her breath. Lucinda Blaylock, who had only that day brought licorice whips to school and refused to share, tripped in the schoolyard and came down face-first in a puddle of black mud.

When she was seventeen, she made a poppet out of cotton cloth stuffed with a man's monogrammed handkerchief and anointed it with certain oils before giving it the name of the young man to whom the handkerchief belonged. She carried it next to her heart for a month, and for all that month the man would dance with no one but her. Then she took back the name and burned the poppet, and let the man go.

1862
Belmont, Missouri

KEVIN Mulcahey was carrying a torch in his hand when he found the dead rebel, even though it was broad daylight.

He was alone on a road in Belmont, Missouri, the rest of his squad being likewise engaged in burning the rebel camp—a waste of perfectly good food, thought Kevin. But in the manner of the army the general had told the colonel to burn everything, the colonel had told the major, the major had told the captain, and so on, until the sergeant told Private Mulcahey, and, there being no one further to tell, the deed had to be done by himself and his mates.

The rebel wore an officer's uniform with a major's insignia. He had a bullet hole in his left breast and another in his left temple. He was dead and no mistake.

This wasn't the first dead man that Kevin had ever seen and he knew exactly what to do. He approached the dead major and made a cross on what was left of his forehead, saying, "Into Thy hands I commend thy spirit."

Kevin had studied for the priesthood in Ireland before he decided that if he was going to sleep with a woman he wanted to marry her and that he was of a mind to someday sleep with a woman, and so had shipped on a packet, jumped ship in New York, and made his way to Cicero, Illinois, where he made a living carving tombstones. At the commencement of hostilities he joined the 27th Illinois Infantry for lack of something better to do, which brought him eventually to this dusty road on the seventh of November in 1861.

Having given a benediction, Kevin looked more closely at the rebel. The dead man had a sword in his right hand, the blade smeared with blood.

"Gave as good as ye got, did ye?" Kevin said, and pulled the sword from the man's grip. Then he unbuckled the sword belt to take the scabbard and patted down the major's pockets for tobacco or gold; either would serve.

Neither was present—only a packet of letters addressed to "Maj. Edward Butler, 11th Louisiana" in a feminine hand, some Confederate scrip, and naught else. Mulcahey was standing there still when Sergeant Dusselman, a Pennsylvania Dutchman who had worked in a butcher shop in Chicago until the war came along, shouted, "Mulcahey, you damned Mick! Quitcher gawkin', man, and look lively. We're pulling out. Back to the assembly, damn your eyes," then passed on along the line, shouting curses and imprecations to the others in the squad as he went. "We're on the boat out of here in jig time, damn you all, or you'll be left behind and no sorrow to me."

With that, Private Mulcahey trotted off the road, put his torch to a hayrick, then headed north toward the rest of his regiment. To the south, the rattle of musketry told him that the rebels were coming again. Across the river, the booming of the water battery at Columbus increased in tempo.

Mulcahey reboarded the boat that had taken him to Belmont that morning. By nightfall he was back in the camp at Paducah, and counting himself lucky, for not everyone had come back.

Belmont itself hadn't been much to speak of, only three shacks at the ferry landing. The rebel camp hadn't been much either: tents enough for three thousand men, stores and supplies. But now Mulcahey had seen the elephant. He'd heard guns fired in anger, had seen men fall, didn't himself run away, and had a bit of booty to show for the day's work.

"Sergeant sees that, he'll take it away," said Padraich Connor, sitting on a nail keg in the company street by the tent he shared with Mulcahey. He was Boston-born, a rawboned redhead next to Kevin's wiry build and black-Irish coloring, who'd come west to Illinois with the railroads. "Too fine for the likes of us."

"Never a bit of it," Mulcahey replied. "Sergeant's seen it already and not a word he said." He had a rag and a bucket of water and was polishing the blade. The blood was dried on and hard to remove, but he kept at it, rubbing from the hilt to the point and back, his strong fingers clamped hard around the steel.

"Why do you suppose himself had us burn the camp?" Padraich wondered.

"Couldn't take it with us and couldn't leave it for Johnny, so we burned it there and came away. A good day, for we're both still on our feet."

"If you paid as much attention to your own gear as to that blade, you'd not be standing extra guard," came Sergeant Dusselman's voice from behind the pair of them. The bugle notes of the tattoo drifted through the camp as he spoke. "Tomorrow at inspection, you be sharp."

Kevin and Padraich turned to the sergeant. "Indeed, Sergeant," Kevin said, touching his eyebrow with his right hand. "So we shall."

"Tempting fate," Padraich whispered in the dark of their tent later. "He'll find something. Watch the bastard do it."

"Your problem," Kevin replied, "is that you think that one way to pass a day is worse than another. What can he do to us? Make us sleep in the mud?" With that he rolled in his blanket and fell asleep.

The morning quarters for inspection proved as bad as Padraich had expected; Dusselman had indeed found them both "Untidy in Accouterments" and given them each four hours of fatigue.

"Unhappy that he came away empty-handed," Kevin said when they were done and had returned to the company street. "Jealous, the man is."

"Things of this world don't matter to you, do they?"

"Not a bit of it."

"Then give him the damned sword. You didn't kill the reb yourself, did you?"

"I'm not certain sure that I killed any man yesterday, Padraich darling." Kevin reached under his bedroll and fetched forth his captured sword. The blade was stained as brown as it had been the night before.

"I thought you'd spent the night cleaning that."

"Ah, it was dark," Kevin said. "Missed a bit."

"You sure it isn't rust, from laying it on the ground?"

It wasn't rust. Before tattoo that night Kevin had the blade shining bright again from point to pommel. In the morning, when he pulled the sword from the scabbard, it was as stained as if he had never taken cloth to it.

1862

Pea Ridge, Arkansas

THIS was the foulest night that Lieutenant Younger had seen in a while, and he'd grown up on the western border of Missouri and knew a bit about foul weather. Charlie Quantrill had given up his guerrilla operations for the winter, so Younger had gone east with his new commission in the Confederacy's regular army to pass the time in productive fashion until the season for riding in Kansas came again. Now he wasn't too sure that leaving Quantrill had been a good idea. The night was black, with a freezing rain falling, and he and his company had been on the move with no rations for the past two days. At least—being an officer—he was on horseback and not on foot, but Lieutenant Younger wasn't certain how long the horse was going to last either.

General Van Dorn had called the officers together while there was still daylight and told them they were going to hit the Federals in the rear by taking a cutoff. Then Van Dorn, suffering from chills and fever, had gone back into the ambulance wagon he was traveling in and left it to the junior officers to do his bidding.

Another horse was approaching in the darkness; Younger could hear the animal blowing behind him,

and the faint jingle and creak of saddle and tack. Letting his men march on, he reined up and turned to
greet the newcomer.

In the freezing dark, the rider was little more than a
looming dark grey shape. Younger could see the man's
breath, see the horse's breath, see his own breath, but
he couldn't see the newcomer's face. He thought from
the way the stranger sat his horse that he was an older
man, heavy in the way that some old men get heavy
without getting fat.

"Help you, friend?" Lieutenant Younger said, when
they were close enough to speak without shouting.

"Looking for a fellow," the stranger said. He wore
a wide-brimmed, light-colored hat that shadowed his
features, and his voice had a touch of Missouri to it
and a touch of somewhere else that Younger couldn't
place. "Name of Coleman Younger. I hear he's with
this column."

"You found him. I'm Cole." He was too polite, after
the way of the Western frontier, to ask the stranger's
name, but if pressed he'd have to own that he was
curious.

"Call me Mr. Thomas," the stranger said, as if reading the lieutenant's thoughts. "Figured it might be
you. We have a lot to do tonight, and you have a lot to
learn, if you're willing."

"If it's for Missouri," Younger said, "I'm always
willing."

"I thought you might be," said Thomas. "I'm glad to
know I wasn't mistaken. I'll bring you to General Pike.
He's expecting you."

"Do you have some orders for me, sir?"

"General Pike is a little ways ahead of us, with his
Cherokees; I've already spoken with him about help-

ing out with this." Thomas regarded Cole from under the brim of his hat. "The first thing you'll have to do is become a Freemason."

In spite of himself, and in spite of the cold and the darkness surrounding them, Cole laughed.

Thomas caught the wave of mirth and laughed as well. "You're thinking 'A Mason in Dixie,' right about now, aren't you?" he said.

Lieutenant Younger stopped his mirth abruptly. "You can read my mind."

He'd always known that there were men and women who could do something like that with a touch of their bare skin against another's, just as there were some who could tell the history of an object when they held it in their hand; but he'd never heard of any who could do such things without any physical touch at all.

"I promise you faithfully that I can't," Thomas said. "No matter what it seems like. And I promise that someday you'll understand. Now if you'll come along with me, you have a long night and a bloody day ahead of you."

Thomas led the way, riding off into the woods at a slight angle to the line of march—but purposefully, like a man with a fixed destination in mind. Cole followed him, and thought as he did so that a man didn't need any particular gift of foresight to know what was ahead for tomorrow. There was a big fight coming, and the only real question was who would live and who would die.

After perhaps a quarter hour's riding through the icy rain, Cole saw lantern light ahead of them amid the trees. When they drew closer, he saw that the lantern was hanging from a tree branch, and that a man was waiting there, dismounted, in its glow. He wore a general's uniform; from that, and from his flowing dark hair and beard, Cole knew that this must be General Pike, who had brought three regiments of Cherokee cavalry to the war. Thomas dismounted and tied his horse to a tree limb, and indicated to Cole that he should do the same.

"Well, Mr. Thomas," General Pike said, when they were done. "What do you have for me?"

"McCulloch and McClintock will be dead before they know it," Thomas said to Pike. "Then Colonel Hebert's captured, and the whole chain of command collapses after that."

"Not a day that's going to cover Van Dorn with glory, eh?"

"No," Thomas said. "Very little glory to go around. You'll do all right, though."

Cole found their way of talking strange—speaking of death and destruction with the ease of old friends, and discussing the events of the battle to come like a pair of Mexican War veterans sitting on the porch and trading yarns about the siege of Vera Cruz—but he knew better than to remark on it. He'd been in the regular army long enough by now to know that generals were allowed to indulge their oddities of dress and demeanor when private soldiers and subalterns were not.

Instead he cleared his throat and said, "Mr. Thomas says I'm supposed to learn something from you, sir."

"You told him that, did you?" Pike asked Thomas.

"I did. He can't learn everything in one night, but he can learn enough to teach himself what he needs to do later."

"Then I suppose I should set him properly on the

road," Pike said. He rounded on Cole and fixed him with a piercing stare. "Have you come hither seeking instruction?"

Cole thought that it sounded like a formal question. He didn't know what he was meant to answer, so he settled on the truth. "I suppose I have."

"This is a matter of some urgency," Thomas said to Pike. "By dawn this young man must be an entered apprentice."

"He'll be that and more," Pike replied. "Fetch the hoodwink." The general turned back to Cole. "Only a few learn what you're about to. I'm relying on Thomas; he tells me that you can be instructed. Turn back now if you think he's wrong, because if he *is* wrong, then by dawn you'll be dead."

Cole looked over at Thomas. The old man's expression was shadowed by the brim of his hat, and unreadable in the lantern glow—no guidance there, Cole thought, as to what he should make of these strange doings on the eve of battle. But he had never been one to turn back from a bet or from a dare, and he saw no point in changing things now.

"I'm ready, sir," he said.

"So be it."

Thomas handed over a black canvas bag to General Pike, and the general slipped it over Cole's head. The dark, close-woven fabric blocked all of the light from the lantern, and the bag smelled like it had last been used to carry potatoes and onions—further proof, Cole supposed, of the hasty and improvised nature of the current proceedings.

He felt something sharp pressing against his throat. A knife, probably; Pike and his Cherokees favored the heavy fighting blades.

"You have an oath to swear," Pike said, from close up. Cole thought that it was probably him with the knife. "Are you willing?"

"I said already that I was."

The point of the knife moved away from Cole's throat, then came back again to press against his cheek, just above the angle of his lower jaw. The pressure—not hard enough for pain or damage, but enough to make the knife's presence clearly known— moved upward over Cole's cheek until the point of the blade rested on his right eye. He fought down the urge to blink, and hoped that the general had steady hands.

"Supplicant," Pike said, "take one pace forward."

Thomas and the General had spoken as though they had a use for him, Cole thought, feeling keenly aware of the pressure of the knifepoint. He would have to trust that they didn't intend to half blind him first.

He stepped forward, and was not impaled.

1840

Springfield, Illinois

MERCY Levering had no use for the young men of Baltimore. One and all, they disappointed her. She had not attempted any influence upon them since her first experiment had shown her the unsatisfactory nature of the resulting attachment; there might be some people who would take love's hollow simulacrum if they could not achieve its reality, but she thought she had more pride than that.

Nevertheless, she knew that she must, in time, find a suitable man and marry him. No other course lay open to her—a woman of her family and breeding could not expect to support herself by baking or nursemaiding or taking in laundry, and even turning schoolteacher would be enough to shock her family into opposition.

Just as well, she told herself, with only a little bitterness. *I should make a dreadful teacher.*

Letting herself dwindle by degrees into spinsterhood—falling by default into the role of an old maid, the family's never-married daughter—was likewise insupportable. Men would laugh at her; women would pretend to pity her, and would make catty remarks about her as soon as her back was turned. And if, someday, word should happen to get about that Miss Mercy Levering knew more than she ought to about some things . . . well, a lone spinster was more vulnerable than a respectable matron to charges of having misused that knowledge.

To her brother in Springfield, Illinois, she wrote none of this, only stating that the bachelors of Baltimore were dull sticks without an ounce of liveliness to be shared amongst them, and that if the same were true universally then she was of a mind to despair of men altogether, and live alone in a cave like an anchoress of old.

Her brother wrote back, inviting her to come to Springfield for an extended stay.

Mercy packed her bags, well pleased with the result of her effort. What need was there, after all, for influence or compulsion, when people reacted so predictably to the slightest and most indirect of ordinary suggestions?

Springfield, when she arrived for her visit, proved all that she had hoped. The city might be not yet fifty years removed from the savage wilderness, but the newly finished state capitol building, with its classical dome and its Grecian columns, proclaimed Springfield a civilized place meant for the carrying out of serious business. Next to Maryland, however, Illinois was a young state, and the men who carried out its business were likewise young, and full of ambition and energy . . . not dry timber, but wood still green and growing.

She was not, she learned from conversation with her brother, the only young woman from the south who had traveled to Illinois for relief from the tensions of life at home. The younger sister of Mrs. Ninian Edwards had come up from Kentucky to spend some time away from an unfriendly stepmother, and Mrs. Edwards was pleased to invite Miss Levering to an afternoon social held in her honor, in the hope that Mercy and the sister would become friends.

Mercy accepted the invitation. As an attempt to compel her regard, it was bound to fail; her own gifts were too great for it. But she believed that her goodwill was being sought without malicious intent, and she was made curious by the effort. What sort of person, she wondered, was this Mary Todd of Lexington, Kentucky, and why would her sister think that she needed a friend?

She found out the answer soon enough. The gathering at Mrs. Edwards's house brought together a number of young unmarried women, as well as a few of the town's livelier matrons, and Mercy was pleased to discover that their talk amongst themselves was not all of males and matrimony. They lived in the busy capital of a rising state, and those few among them who were not interested in politics for its own sake nevertheless understood that it was the consuming interest of just about every ambitious young man in town. Among those women who spoke of the up-and-coming lawyers and legislators of the town with genuine interest was the visiting sister, Mary Todd.

Mary was a dainty little thing, plump and rounded where Mercy was slender and unfashionably tall, and her glossy dark hair was the color of a chestnut roasting on the hearth. She had gracefully sloping shoulders and small expressive hands—again in contrast to Mercy, whose hands were strong and capable and whose shoulders were almost mannishly square—but the single most notable thing about her, in Mercy's opinion, was her eyes. They were dark brown, almost black, with enormous pupils. Mercy had thought in the first moments of her acquaintance with Mary Todd that the other young woman was perhaps a slave to some drug. Then, driven anew by her curiosity, she looked deeper and saw the truth: Mary Todd was a sibyl, one of the rare few burdened with a strong gift of the true sight.

Most men and women with the sight had only a touch of it, a handy knack that might come to play in moments of high crisis, or that could be called forth with the aid of ceremony and ritual. But for a born sibyl, the sight was a constant and ever-threatening presence that could be neither controlled nor escaped. They were highly valued for their insight, and much sought after by those who would rise high or take great risks; not a few of them eventually went mad.

Begin as you mean to go on, Mercy admonished herself. The first thing she said to Mary Todd, once they were left alone after the introductions, was, "I don't want you to tell me my future. I also don't want to know anything about my present or my past that I can't find out myself just by asking."

"You put up a very strong wall. It would take a great deal of work to bring your secrets out from behind it."

"I like my secrets right where they are," Mercy said. "It's nothing to do with your gift, you understand. Just my own privacy."

"If I say that you have your own gifts, I won't be telling you anything you don't already know." Mary smiled. The change in expression made her whole face look sweeter and—for the moment—happier. "I see you, Mercy Levering, and you see me; and nobody else truly sees either of us."

Mercy found herself returning the smile. "Clearly, then, we're bound to be either mortal enemies or the fastest of friends. And since I, for one, didn't come north to make enemies—"

"—friendship it is, then," said Mary Todd. Her smile turned somewhat wistful. "Though I warn you, I don't always make the easiest of friends."

"The same thing could be said of me, and with more cause," Mercy said. "But if you're not afraid to take the risk, then neither am I. The young men of Springfield won't stand a chance against us."

1862

Pea Ridge, Arkansas

B y the time dawn came the next morning, Cole
Younger was convinced of two things: first, that
the day ahead of him was going to be longer
and bloodier than most of the army expected; and
second, that General Albert Pike was a mighty strange
man.

The first was plain common sense. He'd done
enough riding with Quantrill in Missouri to have
learned a bit about what war was like, which was
something you couldn't say about most of the men in
the Missouri State Guard or even about their officers.
Volunteers and patriots all, and Cole respected them
for it, but that didn't mean he put much faith in their
understanding of the situation.

The freezing rain that had been falling during the
first part of the night had turned to snow in the early
hours before sunup, and now the landscape all around
lay powdered over in white. According to the map
Cole had seen in Colonel Gates's tent before all the
marching started, the road ahead of them was called
Telegraph Road, and it ran along the wooded shoulder
of Pea Ridge toward the town of Rogers. The snow
that dusted its rutted surface was fast turning to grey-

brown slush under the boots of Confederate soldiers and the hooves of Confederate horses.

Cole felt sorry for the infantry. His toes had turned to frozen lumps of meat sometime between the end of the rainfall and the start of the snow, and he was on horseback, with no need to put one foot before the other. The infantry, shod in ill-fitting boots, some not shod at all, were in worse case. The cold mud stirred up by their marching feet seeped in through the cracks and the seams of their boots and turned their feet to ice inside the leather. Those less fortunate marched barefoot and left bloody tracks in the snow behind them. Some of them, he knew, would find their consolation in the thought that the enemy, wherever he might be bivouacking for the night, was suffering as well; others merely grumbled and endured. They'd all have their chance to warm up later, though—Confederates and Federals, cavalry and infantry alike—when the guns began to speak.

The second thing Cole Younger was certain of, this frozen morning before battle . . . well, if he hadn't seen the proof of it last night with his own eyes, he'd have thought that Pike and Mr. Thomas were playing him for a damned fool.

That a man could live in two places and times at once —"or even three," Thomas had said, and smiled like he was laughing at his own joke, one that Cole wasn't quick enough off the mark to understand— wasn't something that Cole had thought to be possible. He knew that fortune-tellers and witch-women and hoodoo-men could see the future sometimes, in scattered bits and pieces that usually didn't make sense enough to be useful; and he'd met dowsers and mediums who could catch glimpses of the past if they happened to touch the right object or stand in the right place at the right time. But even for folks like that, "now" was the only time in which they had a physical body and a real presence; outside of "now," they couldn't ride a horse or embrace a woman or even cast a shadow.

Pike and Thomas, though, they knew about things that witches and hoodoo-men couldn't even dream of. "Esoteric disciplines," Pike had called them, rolling the big words around on his tongue like good sipping whiskey. "The fruit of years of study and practice. I myself am a scholar of sorts; but Mr. Thomas, here, is a genuine adept. As you must yourself become."

"General," Cole had said, "I'm honored and I'm mighty flattered by the trust you want to put in me . . . but I'm called many ways at once already, what with the war and all, and I can't say as I'd be able to do justice to it."

"That's all right, son," said Thomas. "We've taught you enough to get you started, and when the day comes around that you have the free time and the quiet for it—and you'll know when that day is—you can think back on the lessons and practice them all that you want."

Pike dismissed Cole then; but as he turned to go, he saw again how Mr. Thomas smiled as if at some private joke. Mighty strange men, the both of them, he concluded, as he reflected upon the conversation. He would have to think more on his words with them later, if the fortunes of the day granted him a "later" to do his thinking in. Meanwhile, he had other business to take care of.

Resolutely, he put the night's events out of his head and made himself ready for the coming battle, moving into position along Telegraph Road with the rest of the Missouri volunteers. The road itself wasn't wide enough for anything besides hard marching to get into position. For fighting room, the army had to spread out, the infantry off to the right along the slope of the ridge, Colonel Gates and the cavalry—and Cole himself—on the other side, off to the left.

The Federals were somewhere up ahead in the valley. Colonel Gates said that General McCulloch's men would be hitting them hard from the other end of the valley. That was the reason for their own cold, night-long march around behind the ridge. The general aimed to take the Federals from two directions at once.

Cole thought that Colonel Gates was putting a lot of faith in something that was going to play out where none of the Missouri men could see or hear it, or even know what had happened until it was too late to change anything. But he didn't see that Colonel Gates had much choice in the matter either; a colonel had to salute and say "yes, sir" whenever a general had a plan, no matter what he thought about it, and once he'd made up his mind to go along he had to speak to the troops as though he liked it.

About eight o'clock, the order came to advance. It wasn't so bad at first, just riding forward along Telegraph Road with the rest of the cavalry, the sound of hoofbeats and the jingle and creak of harness making a pleasant rhythm in the chilly morning air. Behind them, the sun was up high enough to warm Cole's back, a pleasurable sensation after the snow and ice of the night march. He might almost have enjoyed the ride, except for the faint prickling all along his nerve ends that wouldn't let him forget there was a whole other army out there, filled with men dedicated to the principle that secessionists in general, and Thomas Coleman Younger in particular, ought to be shot down dead.

The Federals wouldn't have much trouble finding him either—moving out with a whole army was a long ways different from riding with a band of Quantrill's raiders. Noisier, for one thing, and a lot easier to spot from a distance, what with the morning sun glinting off of bayonets and gun barrels and saddle tack in quick unexpected flashes of light all up and down the road. If the Federals had put scouts out anywhere, they'd soon know what was coming, and only a damned fool wouldn't have sent out scouts.

Cole had already seen enough action to know that being a high-ranking officer didn't stop a man from being a fool; he also knew that no good was likely to come of counting on other people's stupidity. He thought again about Thomas and General Pike, and their assertion that a man could have a physical existence in more than one place and time. He didn't think General Pike could have mastered those esoteric disciplines of which he spoke so highly, because if he had, he'd have spent last night walking up and down the next day's battlefield and spying out what was bound to happen, instead of hearing about it secondhand from the mysterious Mr. Thomas.

The Federals didn't have any such disciplined men amongst them either, he thought, or there would have been attacks and ambushes and deadly barricades all along the night march, and death waiting at sunup. It seemed likely, when Cole thought about it, that military life was too busy and too full of sudden changes to leave a man time for practicing the sorts of skills that required quiet and leisure in order to learn and carry out.

A quick, rattling burst of gunfire from the thickets up ahead broke Cole out of his half-reverie. There would be no more quiet and leisure this morning—the battle had begun.

Noontime rolled around, and late afternoon. Cole was hungry, thirsty, dismounted, and dog-tired. He expected he'd find his gear again if he lived through the rest of the day without getting himself killed or captured, and if nobody on the Confederate side got routed so badly they had to leave everything behind them in the rush. The prospects for supper didn't look so good, though. Their own supply wagons were quite a ways behind them, and even if they hadn't been, nobody was going to break off from a hot fight to brew some coffee or fry up a rasher of bacon. Maybe if the Federals routed, they'd leave their supper behind for the victors.

So far, the day had been a mess of marching and countermarching, of getting hammered hard by the Federal batteries up along the high ground, then cheering when the Confederate guns hammered back and the Federal artillery fell silent. Taking the high ground a while later hadn't been as exciting as Cole thought it would be. The only things he'd found when the cavalry reached the top of the hill were a couple of broken caissons and some dead horses. War, Cole had decided, was a powerful waste of good horseflesh.

The fighting slacked off for a while after that, but now Cole thought it might be heating up again. He could see the colonel talking to the major, which meant that any moment now, the major would be talking to the captains and the lieutenants—Cole included—and telling them what the general wanted the army to do.

Sure enough, here came the major. "Get ready to advance on Federal positions at the Elkhorn Tavern when I give the order," he said. "Listen for heavy firing on our left; it won't be long then."

And it wasn't much longer, at that, before the sounds of shouting and rifle fire came to them on the wind—just long enough for Cole's mouth to get that much drier and his stomach that much emptier, and for his good sense to start explaining to his courage that advancing on foot wasn't going to be nearly as enjoyable as doing the same thing on horseback. Then the bugles sounded and the major shouted the command to advance. The Missouri militia started out for Elkhorn Tavern first at a steady march and finally—when they were close enough that the bullets from the Federal rifles were coming at them like a hive of angry bees, and they could make out the glint of gold braid and brass buttons on the enemy's uniforms—breaking into a dead run.

Hitting the Federal line was like hitting a wall, if the wall happened to have the bodies and the bullets to hit back. Cole fired his rifle at the first blue-clad figure to come up in front of him—a big, square-built fellow with a rust-orange beard along his lower jaw, who went down from the shot with half his face broken open and spilling blood—and smashed with his rifle butt at the next man and the man after that.

A saber came slashing in at him. He never saw the man behind it, only the blade, when the light of the sun going down flashed off the metal and sent the reflected glare blazing into his eyes like a warning. He blocked the cut with the wooden stock of his rifle and the blade angled away, grazing his knuckles in passing. A pistol went off close behind him; the saber fell away out of sight; his foot caught on the body of a Federal soldier who had been standing in front of him only a moment before.

Cole stumbled, caught himself, and kept on going, because the Federals were routing now, turning their backs and running, and the Missouri militia were in possession of the field.

By the time the last light of the setting sun had gone from the battlefield at Elkhorn Tavern, Cole was shivering, exhausted, and even hungrier than he had been at noon. The regiment's supply wagons still hadn't caught up with them—for all anyone knew, they might have been captured at some point during all the day's marching back and forth and around the local landscape—so there was nothing to make a meal out of except the odd bits and scraps of rations that the men had carried with them in their packs. Cole ate his portion, two cold and crumbling biscuits and a sliver of ham, and curled up inside his bedroll on the freezing ground. At least tonight the pickets were some other man's responsibility, and not his; he was free to get some sleep if he could.

As tired as he was, he shouldn't have had any trouble, even with the dirt underneath him as cold and hard as a Yankee's heart. But the day's fighting, especially that last furious melee at the tavern, had summoned up a nervous energy within him that had not yet been fully spent. His arm and leg muscles ached and twitched, and his mind seemed to spin and teeter like a top inside his skull. He would have felt a lot better, he thought, if he *had* taken picket duty. At least then he would have had an excuse for the kind of restless motion that he needed in order to loosen up enough for sleep.

That wasn't going to happen. Wandering around alone in the dark when you were surrounded by men who had their own after-battle restlessness and itchy trigger fingers to contend with was a fool's game. He wrapped his blanket more snugly around him, pulled his hat down to cover his face, and concentrated on taking deep, steady breaths and feeling the beat of his heart.

Thomas had said that awareness of the breathing and of the heartbeat was the first step to learning control, and that learning control was the first step toward the mastery of those esoteric disciplines he and General Pike had been so insistent that Cole would learn. Cole wasn't so sure about that idea; but he did think it might be a step toward getting some sleep.

He inhaled slowly, listening to the faint whisper of his breath in his nostrils, underlaid with the steady march-step drumbeat of his heart, and exhaled slowly again. Then he repeated the cycle, and repeated it again, keeping his mind loose and easy all the while, until he felt the tension starting to drain out of him and soak into the earth beneath.

The voice was hard to hear at first; it threaded itself into the rhythm of his breathing, hardly louder than a thought.

Come to me. Let me see who you are. I need to talk to you.

He thought the voice belonged to a woman. Her face and form were only a shadow somewhere in the dark recesses of his mind; he would not have been able to identify her if he saw her in the real and present flesh.

I am looking for you. I need to see you. We have to talk.

"I'm right here," he whispered, and felt her presence vanish as he spoke. "Dammit."

"Something wrong, sir?" came the voice of one of the Missouri privates, out of the dark nearby.

"No, soldier," he said. "There's nothing wrong. Get some sleep while you have the chance."

For a while longer he lay breathing steadily in and out, listening to the beat of his heart, but the woman's voice never came back, and, eventually, in spite of himself, he slept.

1840

Springfield, Illinois

THE eligible men of Springfield, Mercy found, were much like the eligible young men of Baltimore, save for the fact that she had not known most of them since childhood and could not name most of them as in some degree kin. That advantage, though small, was enough to make her consider her move a success—she would, she thought, decide in time to marry one of them. Even if she had not reached that conclusion, she knew she would have considered Springfield to be a fortunate place, since it had brought her the first true female friend she had ever known, and the first friend who had seen her for what she was.

Mary Todd was, indeed, a friend such as Mercy had never before known. She was vivacious and outgoing, and despite her sibylline gifts, she never lacked for suitors. She had a neat figure and a pretty face, and if her moods were somewhat variable and uncertain, that was something only to be expected. The gift of prophecy was not always kind to its possessors, especially those who could not summon or dismiss it at will—but those who were so ridden by it had oft-times the surest and clearest knowledge. More than one young man of wit and ambition had courted her, reckoning her as good a catch by reason of her gift as because of her position as the richest heiress in Sangamon County, or even the whole state of Illinois. She danced and flirted with them all, and to some of them she whispered a word or two behind her fan, so that their cheeks flushed red or paled to ashen grey, and they left soon after and found other ladies to honor with their regard.

The lanky young lawyer who was a junior partner with John Todd Stuart was nothing special. He had no good looks to recommend him, being beanpole tall and spider limbed, with a face all jawbone and hollow cheeks and a sometimes cynical twist to his long mouth. But Mary looked at him across the dance floor and nodded.

"I'll have that one, I think," she said to Mercy, behind her fan.

"You don't mean it," Mercy said.

"Yes, I do."

"He's too poor and he's too tall and he's peculiar-looking to boot."

"They say he has the sharpest legal mind in the state," Mary said.

"You can't kiss and cuddle with a legal mind," Mercy felt obliged to point out. Not that she herself would have held back on that account, if she were determined to have a particular man for other reasons than kissing and cuddling; but Mary had a need for such things, and Mercy would be loath to see her friend made unhappy by the lack of them.

"Maybe not," Mary said. "But a man who's good for kissing and cuddling may not be good for very much else, and most men don't care as much for the truth as they think they will before they hear it. I believe I'll try this one, and see if he scares away."

What she murmured to him later behind her fan she never said and he never revealed; but Mr. Lincoln neither blushed nor paled to hear it, only raised his heavy eyebrows and led her out onto the floor for the next dance.

1862
Tennessee

PRIVATE Kevin Mulcahey was a forager today. After the battle of Belmont, Sergeant Dusselman had noted his way of finding what he needed, no matter whether it was new boots for a shoeless squadmate or a flitch of bacon to fill out the breakfast coffee and biscuits. The 27th Illinois was making good progress on its way across Tennessee, and liberal forage had been ordered. It was time, Dusselman told Kevin and his fellow private Padraich Connor, for such a pair of handy fellows to turn their talents to the general good.

The day was hot and bright, the sun riding high in a haze-paled sky. An intermittent breeze rose and died and rose again in the heavy air. The clouds of dust raised by the forage party's passing hung about them and settled on their skin and their blue wool uniforms. A long time had passed since reveille; their mouths were dry and their bellies were empty.

Up ahead, Privates Mulcahey and Connor saw a shaded lane, and as the forage wagon and the rest of the men on forage duty followed, they turned that way. The lane led between spreading oaks to a white frame house, with a barn not far away and a fine pair of cows in the field.

"Shall we see what's within?" Padraich asked.

"That we shall indeed," Kevin replied. "For those who have much should share their wealth with those who have little."

They approached the house with caution, even though no one was in sight. The first sign of life that they saw was an open window, and on that window a pair of pies cooling.

"One for each of us," Padraich said. "Like we were expected."

"This war has just improved," Kevin said. "We can pause a moment to reflect on our good fortune."

So the two of them sat in the shade by the side of the house, eating fresh berry pie and licking the sweet purple and red juices off their fingers. As they did so, Padraich asked, "Kevin, my lad, do you hear something?"

"Indeed and I do. I hear a stream flowing and a breeze blowing."

"It's a fine poet you make," said Padraich. "You hear something else besides, am I right?"

"Indeed you are. I hear a woman weeping."

"And are we not to comfort the afflicted?"

"We are, at that," said Kevin. "Perhaps if we tell her we'll be leaving one of her cows, she'll be comforted?"

"At least until the next band of foragers arrives," said Padraich.

"No help for that. But my pie is finished." Kevin stood, and nudged Padraich with the toe of his boot. "So up and away, before Sergeant Dusselman wonders what's become of us."

Padraich rose to his feet. "Besides, someone who makes such wonderful pies may well make fine bread, and the lads will be happy to see it."

They placed the empty pie plates back on the windowsill. Kevin looked at them for a moment. "Should we pay for them, do you think?"

"You'll make an honest man of me yet," Padraich replied. He slipped a promissory note underneath the pie plate he had just emptied. Then, after wiping his mouth on his sleeve, he picked up his Enfield rifle and followed the sound of the weeping woman around to the back of the house.

There they spied a young lady, scarcely older than themselves. She was boiling laundry in a great iron tub and stirring the wash water with a paddle. From time to time she would pull out the garment that she was cleaning on the end of the paddle, then dip it back again into the hot soapy water with a renewed burst of tears.

"Oh, Padraich, my friend, I fear we have come at a bad time," Kevin said. "For yon colleen appears to be washing a bloody shirt."

"Which presupposes the wearer not to be far off," Connor said. "And a Johnny Reb besides. Were we to enter the house, do you suppose the man of it would be waiting for us with a shotgun?"

"From the way that she's weeping," said Kevin, "no."

And he approached the young lady, she in her shirt with the steam plastering the hair to her forehead, and her sleeves rolled up past the elbows, and said, "Your pardon, Miss, but we've come here to buy what we can, and to take what we need."

She did not reply, only let the tears run down her face without stopping.

"Is it your husband that you're weeping for, or father or your brother?" Kevin asked her, but she said nothing.

"Is it some young man you fancy?" he persisted.

Still she made no answer; and Padraich Connor said, "Nothing for it, Kevin, but to go inside and see."

"Our apologies, ma'am," said Kevin, touching the brim of his forage cap with his finger, and backing away.

He pushed open the door to the house with his Enfield. He heard nothing stirring within. Padraich joined him on the threshold, and together, one following the other, the two soldiers walked through the house.

Upstairs was where they found him, a fellow of about thirty with a gingery beard, his eyes deep-sunk in their sockets, closed. He was breathing slowly and noisily. A bandage wrapped around his leg was dark with dried blood, with a crimson trail of fresh bleeding coming from it.

A plate with an untouched loaf of bread lay at his bedside. "Hollo, there, Johnny," Padraich said. "What a sorry place you've come to, and no mistake."

"That looks like an excellent loaf," Kevin said. "I'm thinking that if you were to eat it you'd get well, and you'd come shoot at me and Pat, so into my bag it goes." With that he put the loaf into his forage bag, laying a scrip on the plate in its place.

"That was a cruel thing to do," Padraich said. "What with him dying and all. How would you like someone to do the same to you?"

"Were our places reversed he'd do the same, my lad," Kevin said. "Come on, let's be on our way. Do you see aught of value else?"

They exited the building with their forage bags full, then unlatched the pasture and drove not one but both of the cows before them up the lane, laying another piece of scrip on the ground held down by a rock.

And all the while the maiden washed and wept, and the sound of her lamentations followed them up the lane to the forage wagon.

1840

Springfield, Illinois

THE party was over. The fiddle and the upright
piano were silent; the big downstairs parlor
that earlier had been cleared of furniture for
dancing now stood empty and dark. Upstairs, the
curtains were drawn and the lamps were turned
down low, as those guests who had come from too far
away to return to their own homes, and who had not
found lodging elsewhere, settled down to sleep for
the night.

Mercy Levering and Mary Todd stood in their
chemises and petticoats before the big cheval-glass in
Mary's bedroom. With the house so crowded, the two
girls—being already bosom friends—were of necessity bedfellows for the night. Their gowns, stays, and
slippers already lay discarded on the chaise longue in
a welter of taffeta and kid and whalebone; their cotton
lawn nightgowns awaited them, stretched out side by
side across the foot of the bed.

Mercy freed Mary's rich brown hair from its pins
and bindings and took up a horn-backed brush from
the dressing table to give it the hundred strokes that
insured its luster.

"You danced more than once tonight with Mr. Lincoln," she said. She drew the brush down through the sleek tresses, lifted it away, and drew it down again in a steady rhythm.

Mary smiled. "Yes, I did."

"He doesn't dance very well." Mercy pondered the question. The hand that held the hairbrush continued its steady motion—down, lift, and return. "Perhaps it's because he's so very tall. Though many tall men are quite graceful, so it can't be that."

"No. He isn't graceful. But they're right when they say that he has a clever mind."

"More than clever, I think," said Mercy. "You didn't frighten him away when you whispered the truth in his ear. He could be a rare catch on that account alone." Another long stroke of the brush through Mary's dark tresses. "What did you say to him?"

"You know I can't tell you that," Mary said. "People's private truths are theirs alone. It's bad enough that I can see them, without letting the whole world know."

"If I were to ask you to whisper the truth in *my* ear," said Mercy, suddenly full of a great daring, "what would you say to me?"

Mary's lips turned up. "I would say that you are the friend of my heart, and that if you made up your mind to it, you could do either great good or great ill in the world."

"Fiddlesticks," Mercy said. "I shall marry some man and keep his house and bring up his children. Which may be a good in the world, but I should scarcely call it a *great* good."

Mary stepped away from the mirror. She took the horn-backed brush from Mercy's hand and laid it down on the dressing table; then she took both of Mercy's hands in hers. Her expression, which had been humorous only a moment before, turned suddenly grave.

"Friend of my heart," she said. "Tell lies to the world if you have to, and to me if you truly cannot help it—but do not tell lies to yourself."

Mercy felt her breath catch, and her pulse began to beat more strongly. "What do you mean?"

"You have the power to call others to you, and the power to compel them; and you have the power to bend gross matter to your will. Those are no trivial gifts."

"I haven't done anything like that since I came to Illinois," she protested weakly. "Not for a long time, really." She tried to withdraw her hands from Mary's, but the other girl's grip was surprisingly strong.

"Before you came here you did it—more than once—and the mark is still on you."

"What if it is?" Mercy asked, and this time she let the bitterness show. "I can make a man want to dance with me, but not make him love me; I can take petty revenge on a foe; but those things are nothing, measured against the size of the world."

"And next to the scope of your gift, they are also nothing. You know this, Mercy; I can see it in your heart."

"And you know as well as I do that the world is not eager to let a woman use the gifts that she has."

"Then I tell you, do not pause and ask the world for its permission, when the time comes that you see clearly what must be done!" Mary's eyes were wide open and almost all pupil—the iris barely a thin ring of color around the black—and she no longer seemed to be looking at Mercy, but through her and past her to something in the far distance. "There are bad times coming, very bad times, with the power in them to change all of history to come, and not for the better, either. We cannot let the fear of what we might become stop us from doing what we have to do."

"'What we have to do'— now you begin to make me afraid, when I wasn't afraid before." Mercy tried to put a teasing lightness into her words, but could not banish the betraying, truthful quaver in her voice.

"We should all be afraid." Mary's bosom heaved; she began to tremble, and her eyes, already wide, grew wider still, staring out at the invisible and showing white all around; her face had lost its color. "I'm seeing such dreadful things—death and disunion, the whole country unraveling like a badly knit shawl, the cities burning and the crops in the field put to the torch— Oh, Mercy, I want to stop it and I can't!"

Mercy gathered her friend into an embrace; Mary's whole body was shaking, and her breath came fast. "Be at ease, dear heart; be at ease. You say that I have the power to do great good in the world; well, then, I will study how to stop this thing, and do it for your sake."

"No!" The exclamation came almost as a shout, muffled against the flesh of Mercy's shoulder. "You don't understand. We can't stop it—we mustn't. Those afflictions are nothing, set against the great darkness that I see waiting beyond them."

"What thing? Tell me, Mary." Mercy straightened her back and lifted her chin. "I meant what I said. If you tell me that there is something that I need to do, in order to keep this darkness you have seen from falling over us, then I swear on my love for you that I will do it."

Mary raised her head from Mercy's shoulder and

drew a deep breath. Her face had resumed its normal color, and her eyes had lost their dilation and fixity, and were now brimming with unshed tears. "You are the best of friends, Mercy Levering. I promise I will tell you everything I see that pertains to you and to your gift—and since you've chosen to keep it a secret, then so will I—but I can't tell you now what you should do, because I haven't seen it yet. All I can see is that dark chasms lie gaping ahead of us, both on the right hand and on the left, and that all of our efforts to walk a straight path between them will fail."

1862
Shiloh, Tennessee

KEVIN Mulcahey and Padraich Connor had been camping south of Pittsburg Landing on the Tennessee River for nigh onto a month. Camp life had settled down into a routine, the same as it had done in Illinois, the same as it had in Paducah, where the regiment had camped before Belmont. Sunday was a light-duty day, but that didn't stop them from being up before dawn brewing coffee.

"Real coffee today," Padraich said. "Being camped on the river has its advantages." He had a mess of coffee beans spread out in his frying pan, roasting them over the campfire, and the rich, sharp aroma of them rose up like a promise. "A man could get used to this."

"Did you hear something?" Kevin asked. He'd always been the one with sharp hearing, though he couldn't honestly say whether it was his ears that were better, or his attention, for catching the faint and distant sounds that most people paid no heed.

Padraich gave the pan of coffee beans a shake, the better to turn them over and roast them evenly. "No."

"I thought I heard a drum."

"Maybe you did. There's enough of them about, this being the army and all."

"It's more than that," Kevin said. "Listen—there it goes again."

"If it's important, the sergeant will come and tell us about it presently," said Padraich. "I heard it from the cook who heard it from a messenger who heard it from an orderly that the general himself says that there's no rebels within a hundred miles. Do you think we'd be encamped in open order otherwise?"

Kevin shook his head and left Padraich to his roasting. Then he went back to their tent, brought out the sword that he'd carried away from the field at Belmont, and belted it on. He had no clear idea why he did that, save that it made him feel better prepared for whatever the distant noise of drumbeats might portend. While he was at it, he also fetched the coffee grinder and his tobacco pouch. He might as well enjoy breakfast while he had the chance.

Then he went back over to the campfire, where Padraich held out the pan of roasted coffee beans. "Right on time, and the water's boiling."

"I heard something else," Kevin said. "Something like a growl, a beast in the woods."

Padraich looked around uneasily. "Perhaps there are bears about."

"Bears, the man says." Kevin snorted. "If I were you, I'd put my pack on my back and my cartridge case in order."

"Is that why you're wearing the sword, then?"

"Indeed it is," Kevin admitted. "We've heard nothing from the Seceshes for all the long days, and the prickling of my skin tells me that may be about to change."

"Have you never got the blade clean?"

"Never. Let me show you."

Kevin drew the sword from its sheath. At the sight of the blade, Padraich crossed himself. "Kevin, my friend—what do you see when you look at the steel?"

"Yesterday? I saw a stain that was dried and brown." Kevin swallowed hard. "Today? What I see is fresh and red."

"And none of yours?"

"Not mine or any man's."

Padraich crossed himself again. "That does not bode well."

"It can't be helped," said Kevin, and slid the blade back into its sheath. "Brew up the coffee, Padraich darling, so we can face what comes without yawning at it."

The day was still barely light when they had finished emptying their tin cups for the second time. A thin fog spread along the ground, where the smoke from the campfires barely rose above the level of grass still dried and brown from winter.

"Something's moving along the far side of the clearing," Kevin said. "Maybe the Twenty-fifth Missouri, shifting camp."

"Odd work for a Sunday, and mighty early," Padraich said. He stood and gathered his Enfield to him. "You're the one with the sharp ears, Kevin. Tell me that wasn't a howitzer went off just now."

"I can't do that," Kevin said. As he spoke, the bugle sounded "Attention" and the drums rolled the long roll. "The lads coming out of the woods yonder are all in butternut, so here's where we earn our pay."

"Those are skirmishers," Padraich said. "They can't take our line."

"Maybe not. But there'll be a proper line close behind them."

"Form it up, form it up! With your arms, dress and cover!" Sergeant Dusselman's voice roared out. Other sergeants up and down the camp took up the cry, and not an instant too soon. The rebel soldiers on the far side of the camp were breaking into a sprint.

"Steady, lads, load!" Dusselman shouted. "Ready!"

An explosive shell blossomed amidst the tents. The men who had been at the far side of the camp came running—half dressed, some of them, and putting one foot before the other as if the ground were hot.

"The whole damn rebel army's coming after us!" one of them shouted as he bulled his way through the Federal line. Nor did he pause, but vanished over the hill behind them.

"Gives us more to shoot at," Padraich said to Kevin. A man among those who had formed up beside them fell, clutching at his arm, then crawled away behind the line. "Dusselman can give the order anytime."

"Aim!" came the sergeant's command, an instant later.

"That's more like it," said Padraich. Kevin didn't waste breath on an answer, but took a bead on a rebel in the middle distance.

"Fire!"

A cloud of smoke obscured the field. Even as it swirled and parted and came together again, Dusselman's voice called, "Load!"

Small twigs and bits of leaves drifted down from the tree limbs overhead. Kevin thought that stray bullets must be clipping them—overshots from somewhere, probably from the rebels.

"Present!" It was another voice, not Dusselman's: Roarke, the corporal of the second squad.

"Aim!" Roarke's voice again; and Kevin thought, *Is*

Dusselman down, that we can't hear his great voice bawling any longer?

"Fire!"

This time, when the smoke drifted away, the rebel skirmishers were gone. Instead, the edge of the woods opposite was filled up with a solid rank of grey and butternut. Rebel battle flags flew over them, and a blue regimental banner.

"Who's that?" Padraich asked, but as Kevin turned his head to answer, he noticed that their own line had grown thinner, and that not enough men were lying on the ground to account for the difference. Men had started drifting away, no doubt thinking of their homes and wives. Explosive shells were coming more frequently now, though the rebels hadn't yet found their range.

"Load!" came the corporal's command.

Kevin did so automatically, the long hours of drill taking over where thought no longer counted. His ears were ringing; the repeated volleys had taken most of his hearing, and smoke and the brimstone odor of powder had taken his vision and sense of smell. The distant rank stopped, loaded, presented, fired, then resumed its march forward toward them. Kevin had seen parts of the Federal army, and of the rebels from time to time—but never before, he thought, had he seen so many men all together at once in such a small place.

An officer on horseback galloped past, behind the line—a courier, Kevin guessed, or perhaps the company captain. He didn't have time to speculate long about it. The musket balls whistling toward them were coming closer, and there were more of them. The oncoming line of rebels halted, presented, fired, loaded, then marched forward again. As the rebels fell they closed ranks, but they did not falter from their pace.

The corporal sang out, "On my command, fall out. Fall in on the rear of the crest behind you. Stand by! Fall out!"

"Time for us to cut and run," Padraich said, and turned to lope back up the slope.

Kevin followed him. Now that he was out of line, he could see better, and it was not a sight to fill a man with joy—Rebel soldiers as far as he could see to either side, far fewer men in blue beside him, and among those, many of them running with the look of men who didn't intend to stop. Behind him, a yell rose from the pursuing Southern ranks, a harsh ululating cry of death and exultation.

"Where do you suppose Corporal Roarke intended us to go?" he gasped out to Padraich as they ran.

"Back of the crest, surely, but in truth I'll stop beside Roarke and not before."

"Glad I am to be a private," said Kevin. "Corporal's too hard a job for the likes of me."

Up and over the crest line they went, into a copse of small trees, hardly more than saplings. There stood Corporal Roarke with a color bearer and a drummer beside him.

"Form it up!" he shouted, catching a man who'd gone past him and dragging him bodily to where he wanted to form his line. "Right here! Guide on me!" When he had a sufficient number formed up—most of the squad plus half of another—he called out, "Load!" Then, "One pace forward, march!"

Pace by pace they made their way up the slope, until their heads and shoulders topped the rise and they could see down the reverse slope to their camp. The rebels were closer now, but were losing their own formation as they came among the abandoned tents.

"Aim!" Roarke called. Then, "Fire!" The crest line formed a sort of natural breastworks, providing some small protection from the artillery and from the buck-and-ball that was humming up the slope toward the Federal line. Another volley, and Roarke called, "Fire at will! Make every shot count! Fire at will!"

The line commenced a scattered fire. Kevin was intensely aware of the number of cartridges in his cartridge case, and that every shot fired brought him one cartridge closer to none.

Off to his left, more men were joining the Union line. But the rebels were closer, too. They'd broken ranks when they came in amongst the tents, and that had slowed them, but now they were on the slope, moving, and forming back into a battle line. A hundred yards, maybe less, and they would top the rise.

"Form it up, ye bastards!" Roarke yelled. "And keep up your fire. Keep it up, damn you!"

More men filled in behind Kevin and Padraich, three ranks now and shoulder to shoulder, firing past one another, the reports deafening and the powder smoke everywhere.

Then Kevin heard another voice—Sergeant Dusselman, back from wherever he'd gone, yelling, "Company! 'Tet-shun!"

Kevin stiffened, and brought his Enfield to his side. Then came another voice, less familiar but still well known, the captain himself, who only drilled them when the major was nearby. "Company! Port arms! Company! Right, face! Company, at the double-quick, march!"

And they were running, running—along the slope of the hill, down through a lane and a meadow, to where another line was forming, banners flying, on the far side of a level place. From behind them came the growling roar of another cheer, as the Confederate line topped the hill Kevin and his companions had only recently been defending. Now the rebels were rejoicing to see the Union soldiers run.

But we're running in formation, in good order, Kevin thought. *At least it isn't a rout*. And a voice in his head answered, *Not yet*.

"Company, halt! Dress it up, gentlemen." The captain walked out into the field and called out again, "Left, face!"

The company moved as one, and Kevin was astounded to see it. He was also astounded to see that of the whole company, no more than three quarters, perhaps only half, were there.

"Gentlemen, stand easy," the captain said.

When they did, he continued: "In a few minutes, our foe will appear before us. Today we will show them what manner of men we are, and that, resolute, we cannot be dissuaded from our righteous cause. Today will be long, and bloody, but a trial that we shall pass through to victory. I expect you shall do your duty."

It was a fine speech, for the captain was an educated man as well as a brave one, and Kevin thought it a heartening thing to see him standing so before them, unaffrighted by the enemy.

"Company, attention!" Dusselman called from beside them, on the left. Far away, to the right rear, Padraich could hear a bugle sounding "Assembly." "Hand salute!"

Three explosive shells burst overhead.

Kevin found himself pushing his body back up-right, not knowing exactly how he'd come to be lying on the ground. Away to his left, the men weren't standing, though they were moving; farther left down the line, they weren't moving at all. Dusselman was standing before them, shouting "Load!"—Kevin couldn't hear him, but the sergeant's mouth move-ments made it clear what he was saying. Kevin groped for a cartridge, tore it, loaded and rammed home, then put a cap on the nipple of his weapon.

More shells were going overhead, but they were falling long. The rebels appeared again, on the far side of the clearing, and were met by a volley, with no apparent effect. They returned their own volley, then loaded, and advanced.

"Fix bayonets!" Dusselman called, with lungs of iron and a voice of brass, and the men obeyed. Those who did not hear him saw those beside them doing so, and moved to copy them. Kevin dropped his bayonet the first time, and had to bend to pick it up.

Then it was Dusselman shouting, "Load! Present! Aim! Fire! Load! Present! Aim! Fire!" over and over as the rebels neared. At fifty yards they stopped, while one of their officers stood forward firing a pistol again and again at the Union soldiers; then came a volley from the Confederate line and the rebels came running, leaping through the smoke, and everything was steel on steel, and rifle butts and boots, and at the end Kevin ran, panting, and felt himself lucky to still be holding his rifle, and Padraich ran alongside him among a milling group of men in blue.

Ahead was a supply wagon. Kevin ran up to it.

"Cartridges!" he shouted, and the supply sergeant inside filled his hands with the paper cylinders.

He put them in his pockets, took a long pull from his canteen, and only then started looking for the banner of his company. He found it, and Dusselman there, too, and Roarke—the only faces he knew, other than Padraich and the color bearer.

"What do we do now?" he heard Padraich ask Roarke.

"What the captain said. We do our duty."

Forward of them, toward the sound of firing, more troops were gathering, and a troop of cavalry rode past, guidon rippling with the speed of their passage. The men of Dusselman's squad headed that way, and as he walked, Kevin redistributed his cartridges from his pockets into his cartridge box. He would need them soon, he thought; the rattling of musket fire was getting closer.

"At least we're not being shelled," he said aloud.

"Bite your tongue, man," Padraich replied. "Don't give them ideas."

So the day went—firing, falling back, standing and falling back, watching for a sight of anyone they knew or of their regimental banner and not catching so much as a glimpse of either—until at last they came to a stand of trees where an officer, a lieutenant colonel from an Ohio regiment, gathered them and perhaps a hundred others together. He ordered them forward into a branch of the woods to outflank the rebels on their left, and through the woods they went. It was there that shell fire stopped them. When it was over, Kevin and Padraich were lying behind the trunk of a fallen tree, listening to musket balls smacking into its far side at a hundred a minute, and Kevin said, "This seems as fair a place to rest as any."

The sun had gone to noon and was coming down

again, the air had turned hot, and a multitude of flying insects, impervious to powder smoke, were biting at their flesh. Nor had they a bite to eat and their canteens were long since dry.

"Do you suppose they'll ever get tired of shooting at that log?" Padraich asked.

"Only for long enough to come over and bayonet us," Kevin replied. "As soon as we've taken a breather, I'm for going that way," and he nodded his head back the way they'd come.

"Let's have a bit of a chat first," said another voice. Kevin looked up from where he was lying to see an old man sitting on the log with his back to the rebel lines.

"Holy Mother of Jesus!" Kevin said, and out of habit nodded his head on the name of the Christ. "Are you one of the rebels?"

"I'm not one of that bunch of rebels," the man said. "My name is Thomas, and you have something that I need."

"Begging your pardon, sir," said Padraich, "but oughtn't you to be lying down with us back here? You're liable to be shot, like as not, in the middle of your bit of chat."

"Oh, no," Thomas said. "That's nothing to concern you. A wise man told me once that I wasn't born to die by steel or shot or hemp, and I believe him."

"I wish someone with the power to make it so would say the same to me," Padraich said.

"I can say this much," said Thomas. "You won't die today, not if you stay with me."

Kevin heard the stranger's words and the sound of them struck him with more fear than any shot or shell that day. "You're one of the good people," he said. "I should have known."

"I've been watching you two for a while," Thomas went on, paying no mind to him, and less to the Rebel bullets. "Since you stole the bread from the dying man."

"If you're not one of the good people, then you're the devil and come to take me to Hell."

Thomas looked amused. "You wouldn't be the first to think that," he said. "And after today, hell would hold no surprises. But no—I have a couple of easy jobs for you, that's all. The first is to find that man you robbed and do whatever it is for him that he asks you to do. The second job has to do with that sword of yours."

"Sir?" Kevin said. Whatever Thomas might be—one of the good folk or a member of Lucifer's legions—speaking to him respectfully felt like a good idea

"Take that sword to Washington, and lay it in the hands of President Lincoln and no other."

"Might as well ask me to fly to the moon," said Kevin bitterly. "The army—"

"Do you want to die right here," Thomas asked, "or will you do what I ask?"

"When you put it that way," Kevin said, "I agree."

"Then come along, my lucky lads," Thomas said. "Walk to my left, and stay with me."

"Begging your honor's pardon," said Padraich at last, as they walked together through the woods, now grown silent, "but who are you?"

"Someone who wants to uphold the Union," Thomas said. "As do you. We walk the same path, but we'll part ways here."

He touched the brim of his hat, stepped around a tree, and vanished into the drifting smoke.

Just beyond the last of the screening underbrush,

Kevin and Padraich came to the Union banners. There they turned, picking up cartridges from the boxes of fallen men, and joined the line, only to be pushed back and back until by sunset they stood behind a battery of artillery on the bluffs overlooking the Tennessee.

"One more push and they'll have us drowned in the water," Kevin said. "And there's your fine promise of not being shot nor hanged—worth naught but the wind."

"How do you suppose he knew about the bread?" Padraich asked.

"He's one of the fair folk," Kevin said. "And their ways are not ours, nor have they ever done anything for the benefit of man. Whatever we do, we do his bidding at our souls' peril."

1862
Liberty and Hamilton, Missouri

WE need horses," Quantrill said. The Confederate guerrilla leader was a slightly
built man, with dashing mustachios and a
charming air; his enemies feared him and called him
a devil, but his friends were fond and loyal.

Cole nodded. "We surely do."

They were in a boardinghouse in Liberty, Missouri,
this week, Charlie Quantrill and his chief lieutenant,
Bill Anderson; the landlady was a staunch Confederate and wouldn't take money for the small upstairs
room the two men shared. Cole and the rest of the men
were sleeping in barns and corncribs and tents in the
woods, spread out all over this part of Clay County. A
hard May rain was falling, drumming on the tin roof
and running in sheets down the windowpanes, and
Cole was happy to be indoors talking about supplies
and remounts with Quantrill instead of standing outside in the weather.

"If this were unfriendly territory," Quantrill went
on thoughtfully, "we could seize remounts at need."

"People might take it wrong if we did that here,"
Cole said. "Clay County not being unfriendly and
all."

"Which is why I propose to purchase the needed animals," said Quantrill. "Provided that we can find someone willing to sell."

"Good luck with that. Folks around here may like the Confederacy just fine, but that doesn't mean they'll sell us their good riding stock."

Not, Cole thought, that he could blame them. If he had a horse he liked, damned if he'd give it to the army either.

"It may be necessary to travel outside of the area," Quantrill said, "to a town where the buying and selling of war materiel is commonplace." He paused, then added, "Also, we need bullets and gunpowder."

"We do tend to run through 'em," said Cole. "Only problem I can see is, there's not so much extra around here that buying 'em is going to come easy."

"I know. That's why I have in mind going to Hannibal for horses and ammunition both."

"Hannibal? Are you crazy? That's all Union territory over there."

"It is," agreed Quantrill. "Nobody will look twice at a party of Federal officers purchasing supplies and remounts."

"Federal officers," said Cole. "In uniform and all that."

"You catch my meaning, then."

"I surely do. You want me to be one of your men in uniform."

"I trust you to ride with me clear to Hannibal and not get lost in a saloon or a gambling hall along the way," Quantrill said. "Which, sad to relate, I can't say for most of your comrades in arms."

"If we're caught in Yankee uniforms, it's spying, and they'll hang us for it."

"Are you afraid, then?"

Cole stiffened. "No, sir, I am not."

"Then there shouldn't be a problem." Quantrill regarded him with an earnest expression; Cole judged that having administered the rebuke, the guerrilla leader was now getting ready to spread some butter on it. "I can use you now, Cole. Bill Anderson's my right hand in the fighting, but he's no use for something like this. You, though—you're well-spoken, you carry yourself like a gentleman, and you're good at making friends in new places. With you along, we'll ride right into Hannibal and nobody will notice."

"I suppose you've already got the uniforms," Cole said, resigned.

Quantrill smiled. "That was the first thing I thought of."

"Well, you'd better scrape the dirt and the blood off of them," Cole said. "It wouldn't hurt to have someone wash them either. I've got enough trouble fighting off my own insect life without taking on somebody else's."

It was still raining when they set out for Hannibal two days later. Cole's Yankee uniform fit him well enough, and Mrs. Littlefield at the rooming house had done a fine job of cleaning and mending it. You could hardly tell where the bullet holes had been. Wearing a dead man's uniform still gave him a creeping feeling in between his shoulder blades, though, and he didn't want to think about what the dark-blue fabric might feel like to one of those poor souls who had the genuine touch. Most of the time, folks like that kept their gloves on—it was good manners to others and a kindness to themselves—but he wouldn't put it past the Federals to have one on special duty just to shake hands with people who might be in Hannibal under false pretenses.

Hell, Cole thought, *if we had someone like that riding with us, Quantrill would have put him on handshake duty months ago.*

He didn't know what Quantrill and George Todd, the third man in their purchasing party, thought about the possibility—maybe their shoulders didn't creep enough under the stolen uniforms to bring it to mind— but he'd taken precautions against getting caught that way himself. He'd made sure to pack a couple of pairs of gloves in his saddlebags to wear while he was buying horseflesh and bullets. Polite folks would guess, wrongly but conveniently, that he had the touch himself, and would hold off from friendly backslappings and suchlike out of consideration. The ruse likely wouldn't work against a determined spycatcher, but it would cut down his chances of getting found out by unlucky accident.

They reached the town of Hamilton after dark on the second night. The rain had stopped in mid-afternoon, and the dark fields outside of town were stippled with orange campfires.

"I don't suppose," Cole said, "that those belong to our people."

"When did we ever get that lucky?" George Todd replied. "Those are Federals. Supposed to be a company of the Seventh Cavalry stationed around here."

"Looks like a lot more than a company," Cole said.

"Some of 'em could be fake campfires. It's been done before."

"It doesn't matter," Quantrill cut in. "We're Federal officers passing through town on our way to Hannibal, and we don't need to squat by a campfire when we've got cash in our pockets for a room in a good hotel."

The best hotel in Hamilton wasn't much by the standards of New Orleans or Richmond, but it had crimson velvet drapes tied back with gold swags, and thick, close-piled red carpet on the stairs to the second floor. The stairs to the third floor couldn't be seen from the lobby; the carpet runner there was plain grey drugget and the curtains were red cotton. The rooms were clean and comfortable, though, and the doors all had locks.

"I could sleep here for a week," George Todd said. "We've got feather beds and clean sheets, and nobody's shooting at us."

"We're going to have dinner first," Quantrill said firmly. "People will be talking in the dining room, and we'll be saying nothing and keeping our ears open."

Cole pulled the black gloves from his bag and slipped them on. "So long as I can sink my teeth into a beefsteak and fried potatoes, I'm game."

The dining room was full, mostly Union officers but a scattering of locals as well. The beefsteak was tender, and large enough almost to overhang the plate on either side. Cole was halfway through it, and pondering his chances of ham and biscuits and redeye gravy for breakfast in the morning, when his attention was caught by a motion glimpsed out of the corner of his eye. Quantrill, across the table from him, had come alert like a bird dog catching a scent. Cole glanced sideways without turning his head, and saw a pair of Federal officers coming across the room to their table.

George Todd swallowed; Quantrill said, "Easy, now," under his breath, then raised his voice to greet the approaching men. "Good evening, gentlemen."

The senior of the two Federals nodded at Quantrill and Todd, then at Cole. "Majors," he said. "Captain."

"Is there something we can do for you, Captain?" Quantrill asked.

Cool as ice, Cole thought admiringly; and, *Good thing Todd's too nervous to say anything; he's sweating like a pig.*

"Lieutenant Bronson and I were wondering if we could beg the favor of a bit of the captain's time," the Federal officer said. He looked at Cole's gloved hands. "That is, if I'm right in guessing that you've got the touch."

"Only a mite," said Cole. "Not enough to call myself reliable."

"Any help at all would be appreciated," the Federal officer said. "You see, we're in a bit of a pickle at the moment, the lieutenant and I."

"How's that?" said Quantrill.

"We have a prisoner," said Lieutenant Bronson. "Maybe a spy. But we can't tell if we *ought* to have him, or not. There's been a great deal of suspicious behavior, you see, but never any proof."

Quantrill said, "Have you considered turning him loose and watching him like a hawk until you get some?"

"We wanted to do that," said the Federal captain. "But the colonel didn't see it that way. Said if we thought he was guilty we should go ahead and hang him. But we don't want to do that."

"I don't see why not," Quantrill said. "Even if he isn't a spy, he's probably a rebel sympathizer."

Lieutenant Bronson said, "If we hanged every rebel sympathizer in Hamilton, we'd depopulate the district."

"You may have a point there." Quantrill waved a

hand at Cole. "Take Captain Dykes and make whatever use you can of him."

Cole and Lieutenant Bronson left the hotel and made their way to the local jail, where the prisoner was being held. The jail was a one-cell lockup more suited, in Cole's judgment, to holding the town drunk after a bender; and the sheriff, a dyspeptic-looking sort, gave the pair of Federal officers a dark look, as if he either resented them for burdening his jail with a possible Confederate spy, or resented them for burdening him with themselves.

"What exactly did you catch this man doing?" Cole asked Bronson, as they followed the sheriff back inside the building.

"I'd rather not prejudice your impressions," Bronson said apologetically. "Call it 'suspicious behavior' and leave it at that—but nothing provable, or we wouldn't be asking a favor like this of you now."

"Right," said Cole, and thought, *This is where we see how good an actor I really am.*

"Here we are," Bronson said. In the jail cell, the accused spy sat hunched at one end of a narrow cot. He was a weedy-looking youth, with tow-colored hair and a sparse mustache, and his hands and feet looked too big for his wrists and ankles. He couldn't be more than sixteen, Cole thought; fifteen and barely a bit was more like it.

The boy was also—Cole's heart sank—a regular runner of information to and from Quantrill's guerrillas.

If anything goes wrong here, they'll hang us both.

No chance the boy would fail to recognize Cole; Cole had recognized *him*, after all, and Cole knew in all modesty that of the two of them, he himself was the more memorable. And the chances of the boy being able to keep his mouth shut and not babble the truth in a panic were very low.

"Straighten up, Jake," said Bronson. The Federal lieutenant sounded rough but not unsympathetic. Cole remembered their conversation in the dining room, with its implication that they didn't want to turn the boy over to the hangman. "We've brought someone to see you."

"'m not interested," said the boy to the cell floor.

"It's to save your neck from hanging, kid. Shake hands with Captain Dykes here, and let him confirm your story."

The boy shook his head. "Don't want to. Don't like touchers."

"It's all right, Jake," said Cole. He made a show of stripping the black silk glove from right hand. "You can trust me. I won't hurt you."

The boy looked up at his voice. Cole hoped that the quickly suppressed flash of emotion in his eyes would be attributed by Bronson to fear and not recognition.

Cole extended his hand. "Here. Won't take long a'tall."

With a show, possibly real, of reluctance, the boy took his hand. A trickle of emotion ran down the back of Cole's neck. He wasn't sure whether it was fear or trust or a mixture of both. He furrowed his brow and took deep breaths—it wouldn't do to be too theatrical here, that would be fatal—then let out what he hoped would pass for a sigh of relief and dropped the boy's hand.

"You were right the first time," he said to Lieutenant Bronson, pulling his glove back on as he spoke. "This one's no spy."

Cole followed Lieutenant Bronson back to the hotel, not saying much on the way. The night breeze cooled the sweat that had broken out on his brow and on the back of his neck, and that had trickled down between his shoulder blades, making him shiver. He was glad of the dark, and gladder still that the jail itself had been only parsimoniously lit. If the Federal officer had noticed him sweating, the game would have been up for sure, and there would have been two Confederates languishing in the Hamilton jail instead of one.

When they arrived back at the hotel, the lieutenant apologized profusely for having pulled Cole away from his dinner, and offered to buy him another one by way of making amends.

Cole shook his head. "I'm afraid I'm all tuckered out after dealing with that boy. If I tried to eat anything now, I'd probably fall asleep with my face in my plate."

In truth, it was not his physical energy that had been drawn upon almost to the point of collapse, but his nerve. He had expected every moment that the lieutenant would see through his charade, or that the prisoner would betray him—it would have taken so little, not even calling him by his name, merely the slightest shift in demeanor to relief in place of sullen fright, and the truth would have come out. But the boy had played his part like a trouper, and they'd both gotten away clean.

"Well," said Bronson, "I'll stand you to a steak dinner tomorrow night, and you won't say no to me then."

"I surely won't," Cole said, and meant it. By tomorrow night, he and Quantrill and Todd would be a day's ride away from Hamilton, and Lieutenant Bronson would be saved the price of a meal.

Bidding the Federal officer good night, Cole went upstairs to his room. Todd was already asleep and snoring. Cole wasn't as surprised as he should have been to see the man Thomas waiting for him, his chair tipped back against the wall and his feet on the hob.

"You'll have found that you're becoming a toucher now," Thomas said without preamble. "Comes with the studying you're doing."

"Anything else comes with it that I ought to know?" Cole asked. Todd muttered in his sleep and turned over.

"Doesn't do a man too much good to know the future," Thomas said. "You'll learn that. Oh, and you'll dream tonight. Pay attention."

"You're just full of fun," Cole said.

"Makes you appreciate life," Thomas said. "Food here as good as I remember?"

"Best I've had in a while."

"Then I'll best have a taste of it before I leave. Where I live these days the meals aren't all I'd like, most times." Thomas stood, slapped his hat against his thigh, and left the room, closing the door softly behind him.

Cole undressed down to his long underwear, then got into bed and poked Todd in the ribs.

"Shift over," he said.

Todd complied, grumbling, and was snoring again before Cole had finished pulling up the covers.

Cole himself was not so lucky. He lay wakeful for a long time, going over all the ways that the evening could have ended in jail and a gallows, before finally drifting off to sleep. When he slept, his dreams were troubled. He thought he walked through a dark forest—not the comfortable Missouri woods of home, but possibly the country back in Indian times before so much of it had been logged over and farmed under, full of wild beasts and strange noises. He was looking for something, he understood that much, but he didn't know if it was a thing or a person or a place, or some strange combination of all three.

This is all General Pike's fault, his dream-self thought crankily. *Before I met him, all of my dreams were ordinary as dirt . . . even the ones with pretty girls in them, at least so far as I've had the chance to compare.*

He saw a light gleaming in the distance through the trees. Because the light was the only thing in his dream that wasn't either himself or the forest, he turned and headed in its direction. He half expected the light to blink out, or to move away—this was a dream, after all, and things in dreams were always changing and shifting—but the steady blue-white glow remained motionless as he approached, even while its source remained invisible.

A voice spoke from in the woods near at hand. "Come here. I have to talk with you."

He recognized the voice; it was the woman whom he had heard calling to him the night after Pea Ridge, when he lay asleep on the cold ground of the battle-field.

"I can't," he said. "I have to go find that light over yonder."

"No!" the unseen woman exclaimed. "Not before I find out who you are. I've been looking—I need to know—"

Her voice cut off suddenly, as if she had been snatched out of his dream by an invisible hand.

Good riddance, he thought. *I don't think that she's friendly.*

He turned back to follow once again the beckoning light—only to find, to his dismay, that it, too, was gone. He spent the rest of the night wandering blindly through the dreaming wood, and woke in the morning scarcely refreshed by his sleep, while Todd complained loudly that Cole had thrashed about and mumbled nonsense all night long.

"Mercy, I have had a dreadful dream."

"Do you mean a nightmare?" Mercy Levering asked. "Or something else?" Though she could guess, already, what the answer would be; Mary Todd was wild-eyed and shaking still, even though it was the bright middle of the afternoon.

"A dream, a true dream . . . and oh, Mercy! I do not think I can bear to remember it." She twisted the handkerchief in her hands until the square of cotton fabric threatened to rip apart from the strain. "Such sorrow and desolation, and Rachel weeping for her children and never finding comfort."

Mercy embraced her and let Mary's tears stain the satin fabric of her bodice. The true sight was a heavy weight to carry, and Mercy was glad that she herself had none of it. It was painful enough being the friend of someone who did.

"Maybe what you dreamed of will never happen," she said. "What would be the use of the true sight otherwise, if not to give you help and warning?"

"Only to make me suffer, I think," said Mary, still pale and shaken but more composed now that the storm of tears had passed. "Why else would it give me glimpses on the one hand of pleasures and worldly delights, and on the other of grief and bereavement unimaginable, and no hint of which I should choose if it is not all to go up in flames?"

"I don't know. But you'll be a married woman soon, and I've heard people say that the"—she blushed, but continued—"that the matrimonial bed isn't compatible with the true sight."

"I wish I could believe that," Mary said. "I don't think the true sight cares whether I'm an old maid or a wedded wife, or even a woman without virtue entirely."

"What does your husband-to-be think about it? Have you told him about your dreams?"

"He knows that I have visions."

"Everybody in Illinois knows that. But does he know how bad it is for you?"

A long pause. "No."

"Maybe you should tell him." Then, Mercy thought, there would be two people in Springfield who could comfort Mary Todd when the bad dreams left her shaking.

"I could never—"

"Why not? If he's going to be your husband, it's his right to know such things."

"I'm afraid . . . Mercy, I dreamed of *him*."

"Mary Todd. You're not going to tell me that Mr. Lincoln would ever do you any hurt, because I won't believe it. I can't imagine him so much as raising a hand to you."

"No no no. I dreamed that I wept by his coffin. The whole world was a desert of grief and anger, and I knew that we had made it so."

Mercy drew a deep breath, and uttered a silent

prayer for calm and steady judgment. It was for good reason, she thought, that the prophecies of sibyls were given over for others to interpret. "God is good, and would not distress us with warnings against things that could not be helped. Do you remember, in your dream, whether the world's troubles came from something that you did, or from something that you failed to do?"

"No. Only the sorrow."

"You should tell him everything," Mercy said. "Then whatever he does afterward will at least be done with full knowledge and of his own will."

Mary straightened and wiped away her tears with the much abused lace-trimmed handkerchief. "You're right. I'll do it. You're a good friend, Mercy."

Then for the sake of our friendship, Mercy thought a week later, when the first day of the new year brought Mary Todd a letter from Mr. Lincoln breaking off their engagement, *I hope you remember that you also acted of your own will.*

1862
Hannibal, Missouri

C OLE, Quantrill, and Todd took the train the
rest of the way to Hannibal, leaving their
horses behind at the livery stable in Hamilton.
Purchases of weapons and ammunition made in bulk,
Quantrill explained, could be more easily transported
by rail, and the guerrillas had enough friends in
Hamilton that they could be distributed from there
later without much trouble. Cole would have preferred
to ride—the train cars were too crowded, and if the
stranger sitting across from him wasn't a Federal officer wanting to share the latest war news, it was a soldier's wife with a new baby and a cranky toddler—but
Quantrill hadn't asked for his opinion in the matter.

Cole took to wearing his black gloves all the time,
because they kept the other passengers in the railroad
car from crowding him too much. Quantrill didn't say
anything about the decision, except to cock a thoughtful eyebrow and say, "Good idea." Cole supposed he
was in favor of anything that would keep people at a
distance.

Cole wasn't sure that Todd had noticed the gloves
in the first place.

The train rattled along. The sound of the wheels

on the track and the steady swaying motion of the cars acted as a soporific even on the most nervous and wary. Cole had the inside seat, close up against the soot-stained window, and, eventually, in spite of himself, he slept.

In his sleep, he dreamed that the train had reached Hannibal, and that he left it at the station. He knew that he was dreaming, because the train car and the station both were empty. Save for him, there were no passengers, and no one waited on the station platform. Everything around him was quiet; even the very air had an unnatural stillness and clarity.

In the quiet, a woman's voice said, "Where is it? Is it here?"

He looked all around him, but saw no one.

Then he left the train station and went out into the streets of Hannibal. The whole town was as empty as the station had been. He moved through streets devoid of humans and of animals—not a draft horse nor a tethered watchdog, nor even a half-feral cat watching a mousehole—but strangely full of all the other material things that people bring with them when they come to live in a place.

At first he wandered without purpose, trying to make sense of the desolation. Then, gradually, he became aware that his feet were taking him in a particular direction, and that something was waiting for him there.

"There," came the woman's voice again. "Follow." And again, when he looked for a speaker, no one was there.

He let the dream—because he remained clearly aware that this was a dream and not reality—guide him where it wanted him to go. He went down first one street, then another, then another, all of them empty, until he came to a building with a sign over the door.

ALLEN'S TAVERN, it said. And the woman's voice said, "Here."

He opened the door and went in.

Inside the tavern were only empty tables and empty chairs, and a polished wooden bar with nobody behind it. A naked sword lay on top of the bar. All the rest of the tavern was in shadow, but the single ray of light that slanted in through the front window struck the blade of the sword and made it give back the sun in a flash that was plainly meant to dazzle the uninitiated. Patches of a dry red-brown substance marred the steel.

Certainty settled over him like a suit of armor.

The sword was what he was looking for, and this was the place where he would find it. He reached out his hand—his ungloved hand—to touch the sword, and felt it recognize him even as he recognized it.

I have you, he thought, and let his dream carry him away into ordinary, unfeatured sleep.

1841
Springfield, Illinois

MERCY Levering found fancy needlework
soothing. Her hands and mind took pleasure in the repetitive, patterned motion, and
the projects that she undertook provided her with a
reason to sit alone in silence and an excuse for being,
at times, so deep in concentration that the outside
world barely seemed to impinge upon her awareness.
Today she was sitting by the window in her room, em-
broidering pansies on a pair of bedroom slippers as a
present for her brother's wife, and pondering the half
a score of suitors who had made themselves known to
her since coming to visit Springfield.

She drew the purple embroidery floss through the
fabric and set another stitch. It was time, she thought,
to make a choice.

She had been enjoying the courtship game for
its own sake almost too long, deflecting the attention of the completely unsuitable candidates before
it could fix upon her, and taking care that no young
man among the more likely prospects advanced too
far ahead of his peers. It was a challenge, to do these
things without employing any gifts other than those
of a fair face and her native wit, and Mercy had always

enjoyed a challenge. But if she kept putting off all comers, the game would start to become habit—and that way, she knew, lay waking up one morning and finding that she had grown by imperceptible degrees into the kind of crazy old maid who knew too much about things that she shouldn't and put hexes on the naughty boys who chased her cats.

Mercy did not intend for that to happen; therefore, the game would have to finish before this year's end. One of the young men whom she had not turned away would have to be singled out from his fellows and allowed to advance and declare himself. It only remained for her to choose which one.

She cut and tied off the purple thread and pulled a skein of yellow from her workbasket to ready another needle, mulling over the eligible young men of Springfield as she did so. James Conkling was promising; so was Mary Todd's Abe Lincoln, who hadn't been Mary Todd's since last January—he had a sharper mind than Mr. Conkling, and more ambition, even if his looks were nothing to brag about. He'd been Mary's choice first, though, and Mercy wasn't going to hurt Mary by grabbing him up now that the engagement was broken. Mr. Conkling was better-looking anyway.

The door knocker sounded downstairs. She heard the maid's steps in the front hall as she hastened to answer, and the door opening, followed by voices speaking back and forth rapidly, and footsteps on the stairs.

The maid came to the bedroom door. "Miss Mary Todd's downstairs in the parlor, Miss Levering. She doesn't look so good."

Mercy paused in mid-stitch. "Has she been crying?"

"I don't know, Miss. But her eyes are big, and she's breathing hard, like something scared her bad."

"Bring her up here," Mercy said at once. The maid went back downstairs, and Mercy put the half-finished slippers into her workbasket and closed the lid. If the problem was only Mary's high-strung nature asserting itself—as it did from time to time, usually over minor matters—her friend would be glad to have a chance to recover herself in private. If, on the other hand, the problem had something to do with the *other* aspect of Mary's nature, privacy was even more important. Nobody was ever truly at ease around a sibyl at work.

The door opened again, and Mercy saw that the maid had spoken truly. Mary looked badly scared, pale and wide-eyed and breathing hard.

"Oh, Mercy!" she cried out as the door closed behind her. She rushed forward into her friend's embrace. "Oh, Mercy, it isn't fair!"

"What isn't fair, Mary darling?"

"I told Mr. Lincoln about the dreadful dreams, about how I saw myself mourning him if we were to marry, and he broke off the engagement."

"Yes, dear. I know."

It was my fault, she thought. *I told myself that if he wasn't brave enough to face his fate, then he wasn't good enough to deserve you.*

"And it was hard to do, because I wanted to marry him, I really did. But I thought that if we weren't married, then we would both be safe." She gulped, and Mercy felt her take a long, shuddering breath. "But it was no good, Mercy. Now all the things I see are even worse."

"Worse?"

"I see a great darkness falling over the land." Her voice shifted into the visionary cadence on a rising note of increasing agitation, and her fingers dug painfully into Mercy's upper arms. "I see years passing by while justice goes undone and hurts go unmended—disunity and dissolution and evil power that spreads unchecked—spirits of air and fire bound into engines of destruction and set loose upon the world until the earth cracks and the cities burn!"

"Hush, Mary, hush." Mercy stroked her friend's hair and felt another pang of regret. "I'm sorry. It was all my fault."

Mary pulled back a little. Her face and breathing were calmer now, after the storm had passed, but her voice was still shaky. "What makes you say that?"

"You asked me what you should do, and I said that you should tell Mr. Lincoln about what you'd been dreaming."

Mary shook her head, tearful-eyed. "All you did was give me advice; I didn't have to take it, any more than Mr. Lincoln had to end our engagement." She gave another long, shuddery sigh. "No, I've made my bed and now I suppose I shall have to lie in it alone. But if good and bad alike are bound in the long run to end in sorrow, then what's the use of doing good?"

"We have to trust that it's pleasing to God."

The answer was not one that Mercy herself had ever found satisfactory, but it seemed to ease Mary Todd's heart enough that she dried her tears and—after an hour spent drinking tea and gossiping about matters having nothing to do with either love or prophecy—allowed herself to be sent back home consoled.

Mercy was not so fortunate. She sat for a long time alone, pondering her friend's new visions and the blame that she shared for the broken engagement.

Mary is badly mistaken, she thought. *It was my fault. I gave her advice that I knew she would take, and it turns out that I was wrong.*

My fault, therefore my responsibility, and therefore my task to fix it.

1881

Stillwater, Minnesota

STILLWATER Prison wasn't the place that Thomas Coleman Younger would have chosen to spend the rest of his life in, if his life had left him with any alternatives. Minnesotans were decent folks, and forward-thinking when it came to their jails and penitentiaries, but a five-by-seven cell and silence the whole clock around was a life fit for a hermit from the Bible times and not for a sociable man. He didn't even have quarrels with the other inmates to distract him. Nobody in the prison was foolhardy enough to seek trouble with the notorious badman Cole Younger, who'd ridden with Quantrill's guerrillas and robbed trains all over Missouri and taken more bullets in Northfield, Minnesota, than any man had a right to do and still remain aboveground.

On the other hand, as he had been promised, he did have a great deal of time to think, and—thanks to the rules against speech between convicts—all the silence that he needed to do it in. He had put off experimentation with the art of time shifting for a long while, fearful that his skills, rough and largely self-taught as they were, would not be enough to carry him through, but on the fourth of November in 1881, he resolved at last to make an attempt.

That evening, when all of the prisoners had returned to their cells and the barred doors had been locked for the night, he lay down on his prison cot and composed his mind as Albert Pike and the man Thomas had instructed him. It was time to find out if they had been right, that night in Arkansas so long ago, when they told him that he had the ability to learn.

He settled onto the lumpy mattress and let his mind go clear. For a time nothing happened except that he breathed in and breathed out. Then it seemed as if he were drifting away and falling, falling backward through the bed and through the years, until he came at last to a dark wood.

A woman was waiting there with a lamp. She was robed all in white, and her features were obscured by a fine drapery of the same color, as if it were a bridal veil, or a shroud. "Have you come here to make my acquaintance?" she asked.

"I believe I've already had the pleasure," Cole said, for the voice was that of the woman who had spoken to him in his dreams when he was a young man in the war. "Could you tell me whereabouts I'm standing?"

"We're close by the Wabash River," she said. "Someday this will be Ohio, but right now it isn't."

"And the year?"

"You're at the right time and the right place," she said. "In a couple of hours all hell will break loose up yonder at the army camp."

She started walking in that direction. Cole took step beside her.

"There's one thing I've studied on for some time

without finding an answer," he said. "If I die while I'm doing this—die here in this place and time, I mean—what happens to me then?"

"I don't know whether it's the case that you won't die here," she said, "or that you can't, but in the end it all comes to the same thing. You don't."

"What about you?" Cole asked. "Folks at an army camp are likely to take you for a camp follower—you being a woman and all—and things could go hard with you on that account." He looked at her more closely. "Is there any chance that when I first met you, you were a ghost, and today's the day of your passing?"

She laughed. "We met? Well, it's possible; but I don't find it likely. Are you worried because we're unarmed, with nothing but wilderness on all sides?"

"I'd be happier with my pistol," he admitted. "But they don't let me keep such things where I'm staying."

They walked on through the woods. The trees around them seemed to glow, so that Cole had no trouble making his way. His guide likewise moved forward with smooth assurance. At length he said, "You've been here before."

"Yes, and so have you," she said. "In a dream that you will have had as a younger man."

"I'm always a Younger man," Cole pointed out, and was rewarded by her quiet laughter at the jest, mild as it was. "And you're tying my brain into knots with your talking. I'm only here for the sword."

She looked at him and said, "What sword is that?"

"General Richard Butler's sword. I went looking for it in Northfield, but I never found it."

"I needed to know that," she said, "and didn't know

that I needed to know it. Thank you for bringing me here."

"I didn't intend to do it," he said. "Or so I thought. But I could be wrong."

The smell of wood smoke came to them through the trees, and Cole could hear the muffled sounds of soldiers stirring to wakefulness, and of horses in harness. They were approaching the camp. He didn't like what he saw when he got closer—just one man on watch on the side he approached, and that man sitting at a fire and warming his hands, where the fire would make him night-blind even if he'd been watching out in the direction of the forest, which he wasn't. Cole was proud of his rank as a captain in the Confederate army, and proud of all the fighting he'd done from Kansas to Louisiana and back during the war. What he saw here didn't look like good soldiering.

As dark gave way to dawn, however, the morning racket of drumbeats and bugles was familiar enough, even to the way the damp air muted the ruffling of the side drums. He could guess how men would be waking, breaking their fast and striking their tents and making ready to move out on the day's march— some still sleepy, most of them hungry, and all of them with their minds already half a mile down the way ahead.

"This is when I'd hit 'em," he said to his guide, as they passed through the picket lines and approached the camp itself. "If I was of a mind to do a thing like that."

"Other minds have the same thought," she said. "You need to watch closely if you want to find the answer to your question."

His guide was a fine woman, he thought, but it was

plain she'd never been close to a battlefield. "I won't be able to see much from out here once the fighting starts."

"You can go further in," she said. "They'll see what they expect to see when they look at you. I'm not what they expect at all, so it's time I must be going."

Before he could raise a protest, she had vanished.

A heartbeat later, the wind shifted. Another familiar sound struck his ears, this time not with the pleasant pang of nostalgia—the sudden quick snapping noise of musket fire, and a high, drawn-out cry. *That's no rebel yell,* he thought. *But somebody out there is on the attack and no fooling.*

He moved more rapidly now, wanting to be within the camp before his presence became known to the soldiers there. It was possible that, as his guide had suggested, he was not vulnerable to injury in his current state—whatever it might actually be—but he would prefer not to test it by getting himself mistaken for the enemy. He wished he could remember better what Indian tribes had been fighting against the government's army up along the Wabash in Richard Butler's day . . . Shawnee, maybe?

Tough fighters, whoever they are, he thought, remembering Albert Pike's Cherokees at Pea Ridge. *They can make the Federals run.*

There was gunfire coming into the camp now. It had been a long time since Cole had heard the air so full of lead; he hadn't missed it much. The infantry officers in the camp were trying to form the troops into line, but too late and too slow. They hadn't yet learned how quickly everything could go to the bad.

Well, they're learning it now.

Somehow, in all this tumult and slaughter—because

it was going to come to a slaughter, he could see that already—he needed to find General Richard Butler, and Butler's sword. There were a lot of swords; the officers all had them, and weren't shy of using them. He saw one young officer slapping at fleeing infantrymen with the flat of his blade and shouting, "Form line, damn you, form line!" as they ran.

Another officer, this one on horseback and resplendent in gold braid, rode through the press with his plumed hat waved aloft, urging the infantry forward. *That's probably a general*, Cole thought. *But is he the right one?* The infantry weren't listening to him much, that was for sure. It would have been better if they had, because now there were arrows mixed in with the musket balls, and the war clubs and tomahawks were coming close behind. Forming ranks and firing all together was the only way to beat back something like that, no matter how much smarter it felt to skedaddle.

He moved quickly through the chaos of the camp, eyes open for another man in gold braid and a cocked hat. Nobody questioned or halted him, and he couldn't tell whether it was owing to the neither-here-nor-there nature of his presence, or to the fact that he moved like a man with his goal already fixed. The officer on horseback appeared again out of the mist of powder smoke, riding a different horse this time, shouting "Cowards! Cowards!" at his fleeing troops.

"God save us, General," came a voice at Cole's ear. "This is a rout."

The speaker was young, with only a little gold on his uniform. But the man he was speaking to was older, and wearing gold braid enough to dazzle the eye, if most of it hadn't been all besmirched with gunpowder and blood. More blood ran down the blade of the sword he gripped in his right hand.

"The cannons," he said to the young officer. "We have to destroy them. Take what regulars you can hold together, sir, and see to it."

The lieutenant said, "Yes, sir," and vanished into the fog and the press of bodies. The general, watching him go, swayed a little on his feet. *Most of that blood on him is his,* Cole thought. *But not all of it. I think he's the one I want.*

Another young man emerged from the press of hand-to-hand fighting. His hat and coat had alike gone missing, but his frame and features marked him out as close kin to the wounded General Butler.

"Richard!" he cried out as he approached. "Tom's hurt! I need your help to—"

"Do what you can for Thomas." Butler's legs gave way under him as he spoke. Cole reached out to catch him, but the young man who had come seeking help got to him first, and lowered him gently to the ground.

"I'll be staying here, I think," Butler said.

"Richard—"

"Good-bye, Edward," Butler said firmly.

Edward choked out a farewell, kissed the older man on the forehead, and was gone, presumably to aid the injured Thomas. Butler lay on the ground where he had fallen, drawing rapid shallow breaths and going steadily paler. Cole wondered if he was hoping to die before the Shawnee got to him.

I might be, if it was me lying there, Cole thought. *Or maybe I'd be thinking about how to convince them I was worth taking alive.*

The lieutenant whom Butler had sent to destroy the

artillery came back, looking dirtier and bloodier than before. "We've spiked the guns, sir. The Indians won't have them."

"Good," said Butler. The voice that had been strong and forceful only minutes ago now rang only weakly. "Take the men you have left, and retreat in the best order you can."

"But, General Butler, sir—"

"I'm dying. One thing."

"Sir?"

"My sword." Cole saw General Butler's fingers fumble for the hilt and fail to find enough strength for a grip. "Take it to my brothers, if either lives. And tell them not to wash the blood of the Butlers clean from the blade."

"I will," said the lieutenant, and picked up the sword. The morning fog parted for an instant as he did so, and the blade was limned in a momentary effulgence of golden light.

I see it now, thought Cole. *And I'll know it as soon as I see it again.*

It was as if the recognition was enough to force his presence—material or immaterial, he wasn't sure it mattered—out of this time and place. He fell down and backward into the darkness, and awakened lying on the hard bed in the narrow cell from which he had commenced his journey.

1841
Springfield, Illinois

O F all the skills and usages of her gift, Mercy found the practice of compulsion the most complex and difficult, as well as the most disturbing. Influencing a person's free will required a delicate touch, if it were not to become a mere exercise in brute force; and the latter, at least, she found repugnant. The greater art, to her mind, was to offer up the intended action as a choice only, but to present it in such a manner that the desired response became all but inevitable.

A persuasion, she termed it, when she thought of the matter. *Or a seduction.*

Ever since her first experiments, she had never called upon her gift to direct the actions of another without a certain inward shrinking-away at the moment of initial resolve. Not because she disliked exercising her own will at the expense of another's, but because she enjoyed it too much—and she was almost entirely certain that taking pleasure in such things was both unhealthy and sinful.

Maybe this is how some men feel when they make a conquest of a good woman, turning chastity into consent for the sake of the game.

Still, she had made a promise to Mary Todd that when the time came she would not hold back from doing what was needed. A broken engagement and a reluctant suitor might seem like a frivolous problem to some people, but not when the prospective bride was the most powerful seer in five states, and plagued by visions of death and civil dissolution.

"I swear on my love for you that I will do it," Mercy had said, and she didn't believe in making promises that she wouldn't keep.

She went upstairs to the room that was hers when she visited her brother and her brother's wife, locked the door, and drew the curtains. Then she lit candles to dispel the resulting darkness—four white candles in plain wood holders, one on each side of the room, and a red candle that she set aside for now on her bedside table. When all the candles were in place and burning yellowly, she rolled up the carpet to reveal the bare floor underneath. Taking a lump of white sewing chalk from her workbasket, she knelt on the plain wood boards and drew a circle around herself, then inscribed the necessary names and symbols around the outside of the circle.

Being careful not to step on any of the chalk lines or smudge them with the hem of her skirt, she retrieved the red candle from the bedside table and carried it back with her into the center of the circle. There she knelt again, and set the candle on the floor in front of her. With the chalk, she drew a second, smaller circle around the candleholder, and inscribed more names around its circumference.

She extended her hands above the flame of the red candle and began to whisper the words she had learned from her teacher's books. The Latin came but slowly to her tongue—a woman had fewer opportunities for study than a man, and she had no desire to be thought unnatural for her scholarly interests—but in this matter, exactitude of grammar and vocabulary took second place to a firm intent. The true reason for the use of Latin as a language of ritual was as a necessary restraint: with time and study, or so her old schoolmaster's books had said, the trained mind attained strength enough that to say a thing aloud was sufficient to will it done. Therefore, practitioners of the art as she had been taught it were instructed from the beginning to call upon their gifts in a language they did not speak.

"Latin is but the most convenient for you to learn," her schoolmaster had told her. "Some of us use Greek instead, and a few use Hebrew, and there's at least one scholar at Harvard who uses Finnish . . . even Abenaki or Cherokee would do, if those were the only languages to be had."

"What did the Romans use, if they couldn't use Latin?" she had asked him.

"Etruscan, mostly. But they never wrote any of it down, so all of it is lost."

He spoke as though the loss made him unhappy. But she had never been one to waste regret on things that couldn't be helped, and she didn't care about the Etruscans either, not then and not now. She gazed at the heart of the candle flame and took the deep, steadying breaths with which she had been taught to begin her operations. Carefully, in her mind, she built up the structure of language and grammar that would let her control the expression of her will. Then she began to speak.

"*Nomino te . . .*"

I name you. . .

"*. . . Abraham filius Thome . . .*"

. . . Abraham son of Thomas . . .

"*. . . et te invoco.*"

. . . and call upon you.

"*Ecce mentem sponsae suae Mariae . . .*"

See now the mind of Mary your promised spouse . . .

"*Quomodum te indegit ut in integrum restituetur . . .*"

. . . how it requires you for completion . . .

"*. . . et ea coniunxtus perficeris facta magna . . .*"

. . . and how joined to her you may accomplish great things . . .

"*. . . sed separatim ambo defeceris . . .*"

. . . but apart you will both come to naught . . .

"*. . . et America tota vobiscum.*"

. . . and all America with you.

"*Per nomina docta mihi, et hic manu mea inscripta . . .*"

By the names which I was taught, and which I have inscribed herein . . .

"*. . . iungetur in his rebus voluntates nostrae, et fiat facere debitum.*"

. . . let your will be made one with mine in this matter, and let what must be done, be done.

"*Fiat voluntas mea!*" she finished, letting her voice rise above a low murmur for the first time.

Let my will be done.

She put out the red candle, then the other four, and removed them from their holders, and put them away out of sight in the drawer of the bedside table. The chalk she returned to her workbasket. Last, she unrolled the carpet and laid it back down over the circles and inscriptions drawn in chalk. For greatest efficacy, they would need to stay in place for at least a night and a day and another night; after that, she would need to wipe them away.

Now, however, it took all of her energy to look once more around the room and make sure that no visible traces of her work remained. That done, she undressed and went to bed, letting her discarded garments lie on the floor where they had fallen. In the morning, when she had recovered, she would put them away. But first, she would sleep.

1844

Springfield, Illinois

O N a spring day in the capital of Illinois, Mr. Lincoln walked up the stairs to his third-floor office. The day so far had been a quiet one, with no trial going on at present. The lawyer was of a mind to spend the slow hours of the afternoon going through the papers on the desk he shared with his partner—their office was prime in its location, just above the Federal courtroom and across the square from the capitol building, but Spartan and economical in its furnishings—and looking for things tucked away and forgotten that needed calling to mind.

Mr. Lincoln found the door to his office standing open, and his partner seated at his desk talking with an unfamiliar man.

"Welcome back, Abe," said William Herndon. "This fellow here says he's come a long way to talk with you about the law."

Abe shucked off his frock coat and hung it over the back of a chair, then sat down himself. "How can I help you?"

"The shoe's on the other foot," the stranger said.

"I've heard of you, Mr. Lincoln, and I've come to do you a service."

"I don't recall being in need of anything in particular—but I've been mistaken once or twice, so go ahead and speak your piece."

"First things first," said the man. "Have you ever met me before?"

Abe turned an assessing gaze on the speaker. He saw an older man in plain clothing, big in the chest and shoulders, with hands roughened and scarred around the knuckles; he looked like someone who'd had a strenuous life and been ill-used by some of it. "Not to my recollection."

The man nodded thoughtfully. "Might I have met your father, do you think?"

"He never spoke of meeting anyone who looked like you," Abe said. "If you could give me a name, Mister—?"

"Thomas."

"No. He never spoke of meeting anybody by that name to my recollection."

The older man looked relieved, or at least as if an important question had been answered. "Then I'm pleased to make your acquaintance, sir." He nodded at Herndon. "And yours as well."

"Our pleasure, sir," said Herndon. He stood and moved to the bottle and glasses that stood on the cabinet. "Whiskey?" he asked, and without waiting for answer, poured himself a shot.

"Thank you kindly," Thomas answered, "but no. A man needs a clear head when he's traveling, and I've come quite a ways to meet with Mr. Lincoln."

"I'm honored to hear it," Abe said, and tilted back

his chair preparatory to commencing business. "Now, then. Why, exactly, do you require my services?"

Thomas chuckled. "I'll own to having needed legal representation from time to time, but never in the state of Illinois. As I said, I'm not here for myself."

"I understand. For a friend, then." Abe was no stranger to hypothetical friends; they made talking about things easier for some people, and the truth always came out eventually.

"No. I'm here on your behalf, not mine."

Abe regarded Thomas over his steepled fingers. "And yet, William here says that you have a question for me concerning the law."

"Which I do," Thomas said. "It's a simple one, but it's been exercising my mind a good deal of late. Do you think that states can leave the Union?"

Herndon laughed over the rim of his whiskey glass. "That's not the law, that's politics."

Abe said, "You didn't need to come to Springfield for an opinion on that; any courthouse in the country would have done."

"And I'd have heard a different opinion in every one," Thomas said. "I'm interested in hearing yours."

It was in Abe's mind to ask why, but he was skilled in questioning and cross-examination, and had seen more than one witness turn silent when pushed too hard. Sometimes it was better to go gently and let the answers come in their own time.

"My opinion," he said thoughtfully. "Well, Mr. Thomas, it seems to me that for one state to withdraw from a union when all the others want to keep it together would go against the whole idea of majority rule. That's the principle of the thing for you, if you want it; but if it's practical politics you're after, then consider only that secession is a fast road to anarchy. A state that breaks away from the Union over some disagreement, no matter how justified, will sooner or later see its own counties and regions doing the same thing rather than compromise with one another."

"Sounds like you've already done some heavy thinking on the matter," Thomas said. "Keep it up, and you'll go far."

"Are you trying to flatter me, Mr. Thomas?"

"Not at all, Mr. President. You'll leave Springfield, but you won't come back." With that, Thomas stood and picked up his hat, a wide-brimmed white hat of an unfamiliar cut. He nodded politely to the lawyers. "I'm sorry I can't stay here any longer—but I expect you'll be seeing me again."

He left the room and walked away down the stairs, leaving the two young lawyers to look at each other in puzzlement.

"Well," said Herndon. "That was certainly odd."

Abe nodded thoughtfully. "It certainly was."

"*Have* you ever thought about running for president?"

"No man goes into politics who doesn't think that some parts of the world might be better if he had a say in running them."

Herndon regarded him narrowly. "Does your wife say that you could be president?"

It was on Abe's tongue to deny that the question had meaning—but he was fully aware that the denial would do him no good. He looked at the door through which Thomas had departed, and wondered what the stranger had meant by his visit. "She did mention something of that sort to me once."

"But did you listen to her?"

Abe's long mouth lifted in a crooked smile. "Only a fool would marry a sibyl and fail to pay attention to her prophecies. And a man as homely as I am can't afford to look like a fool as well."

1862
Hannibal, Missouri

HANNIBAL, thought Kevin Mulcahey, was a fine town, with beer to be had there, and hot food that wasn't from the army's provisions, and if the people weren't entirely friendly to the Union, at least they pretended to be. Kevin and his friend Padraich Connor had an afternoon's pass from camp—they being among the lucky few in their regiment who had made the trip back from Shiloh, and newly made into corporals for their pains—while the 27th Illinois was being restored with fresh recruits.

"Don't tell them stories," Sergeant Dusselman said. "You'll just frighten them." He looked over at the new men in their new dark blue tunics, nothing about them faded or stained or mended, and said, "Farmers."

"Then they'll know how to dig," Padraich said; and Kevin said, "That's a mercy."

"Shut your mouths and be on your way," said Dusselman. "Before I forget I gave that pass to you."

They made haste to obey before the sergeant decided to carry out his threat. That evening found them in a tavern, with drinks in front of them and the night outside. The room was a press of soldiers and fair ladies, and if some of the ladies held that name only through courtesy, Kevin and Padraich weren't complaining. They'd seen little enough of women of any kind on the road to Shiloh and back again, and it was a pleasure just to see their forms and hear their voices, all so unlike the roughness of soldiers.

Kevin had his sword lying on the table before him. Ever since the bloody days at Shiloh, he could neither bear to have it out of his sight, nor could he bear to see it, and at night it troubled his dreams and kept him from sleep. Padraich had urged him more than once to rid himself of it—it was good workmanship, despite the rust stains along the blade that nothing seemed able to remove, and ought to bring him a tidy sum—but he always refused.

"Hsst," Padraich said to him, under the tavern babble. "There's an officer coming. Some mother's darling, from the brave mustache and the downy cheeks on him."

Kevin looked up in the direction of Padraich's nod, and saw a man in uniform approaching. He was younger than either of them, but with a captain's buttons and shoulder straps, and he wore black silk gloves in spite of the warmth of the evening. It was like Padraich, Kevin thought, to notice a man's lack of years, but not that he carried himself like a veteran soldier and probably had the toucher's gift.

The officer placed three glasses on the table, and a bottle of whiskey, and said, "May I join you, corporals?"

"No fear of that, your honor," Padraich said. "If that's how you say hello you'll never want for friends." He pulled one of the glasses over to him and uncorked the bottle.

"Meaning no disrespect, Captain," Kevin said, "but may a man ask why it is that a gentleman such as yourself would feel the need to be so generous?"

"It's in my nature," the captain said. "Permit me to introduce myself. I'm Captain Tom Dykes, and I've a mind to share my good fortune."

"Fortune," Connor said, raising his new-filled whiskey glass first to the air, then to his lips.

"Fortune," the captain echoed, filling his own glass and returning the gesture. He pulled the silk glove from his right hand.

"Fortune," Kevin said at length, but left the glass of whiskey untouched and instead drank from his beer. "She favors the bold, or so I've heard it said. But so far, all that I've seen of the bold is their poor murdered corpses, and I'm thinking that Fortune and Death are two names for the same thing."

"You might say so," the captain replied. "That's certainly the road we're all walking down. Some of us just get there sooner than others, is all."

"It's a philosopher the man is," Padraich said. He raised his glass. "To philosophy."

This time the captain didn't drink, only looked Kevin in the eye and said, "How would you like to spend the rest of the war in ease and comfort?"

Kevin looked back at him, disbelieving. "Can you do that?"

"Kevin, Kevin," Padraich said, suddenly alarmed. "Haven't I taught you anything? Never volunteer, and keep yourself where the officers can't see you."

"What place might that be, do you think?" Captain Dykes said. There was no menace about him, except that he reached out and laid his bare right hand over Padraich Connor's. Kevin saw that a thin film of sweat beaded the captain's upper lip. "Some of us can see farther than others."

Padraich pulled his hand away. "Thanking your honor for the drink," he said, rising. "Kevin my dear, let's be off to camp before the sergeant decides that we've overstayed our passes."

"Stay," the captain said, his voice flat and low— compelling, this time, not cajoling. "Listen to me. I only need two things."

Kevin met his eyes. "Speak, then. I'll hear ye."

"The first thing I need is for you to let me touch that sword you've got there."

"And the second?"

The captain shook his head. "One thing at a time. First I need to touch the sword."

"Maybe you do," said Kevin. "But it's mine."

"I can see that," said Captain Dykes. "Will you let me touch it?"

Padraich was shaking his head. Kevin frowned at him and said to the captain, "There's no harm in letting you handle it, I suppose."

He pushed the sword across the table. The captain reached out with his gloved left hand and pulled it closer to himself, and with the same hand drew it an inch, perhaps, from its scabbard. Then he touched the steel of the blade with his bare right hand. What he saw or felt Kevin couldn't tell; his facial expression didn't change, although the pupils of his eyes went suddenly wide.

For a moment, he said nothing. Then he drew breath and said, "Now the second thing. Will you sell me that sword?"

"Why should I do that?" Kevin asked.

"Well, there's the money," Dykes said, and there was a quirk to his mouth that made Kevin think that at another time and on another day he might have had a humorous bent. "Beyond that—so far it's caused you nothing but grief, and it deals out grief and carries grief with it, and every man so far who's kept it by him was either defeated or died with it in his hand."

"A poisonous thing like that," Padraich observed, "my friend wouldn't be doing you any kindness by selling it to you."

"I'm not interested in kindness at the moment." Dykes looked back at Kevin. "How much is your life worth to you today?"

Kevin saw that the captain was serious, and that he spoke like a man with the ability to deliver on what was promised. "My life's not for sale," he said. "But if I were of a mind to trade away this sword for it, I'd ask for nothing less than to be safely out of the way of any more fighting. I fought for two days at Shiloh, and no man can call me a coward for not wanting to see more days like them."

"Safety with honor? That would satisfy you as a fair price?" Captain Dykes asked.

"It would," Kevin said. "Though I doubt you have it in your pocket."

Came a disturbance at the front of the room, and here through the press came Sergeant Dusselman, parting the crowd like a swimmer parting the waves.

"Mulcahey!" Dusselman said. "Connor! Where the devil have you gotten off to? You're wanted back in camp."

"I have a pass," Kevin pointed out. "You gave it to me yourself, Sergeant."

"And I've been looking for you since a half hour after you left," Dusselman said. "Seems you and Corporal Connor are the lucky men. Sergeants you're to be, assigned to the recruitment and training center at Fort Butler, far from the fighting, for the sake of turning farmhands and grocer's boys into men who'll not break under fire."

Kevin felt the hairs rise up on the back of his neck. "And the orders for us came to you tonight?"

"Not half an hour after I gave you the passes," Dusselman said. "Back to camp with both of you. I've orders to see you on your way by noon tomorrow, and be damned if I'm going to have you staggering back drunk at sunup."

Kevin glanced over at Captain Dykes, half fearing that the captain would insist that Kevin's orders met the price he'd set for his life and, by implication, for the sword. But the captain was already gone, and the blade with him.

"The devil!" he said.

"Aye, the devil," Padraich said. "No good comes of dealing with *him*, either."

With that he knocked the whiskey to the floor so that the bottle shattered, and elbowed his way out of the tavern. Kevin followed, feeling chastened and—without the sword—more than a bit bereft, and Sergeant Dusselman came after, grumbling.

Outside of the tavern, Kevin ran to catch up with Padraich, who was walking fast and angrily. "For the love of God, man, what ails you? We have good fortune handed to us on a silver platter, and nothing will please you but to go breaking glass and wasting good whiskey."

"Kevin, ye daft bastard," Padraich said. He kept his voice low, so as not to draw down the sergeant's ire, but Kevin could hear the sorrowful mockery in it. "There's a man at the fair who can tell your weight to the nearest pound just by looking at you. Would you give away your plunder to him, then?"

"What do you mean?" Kevin asked.

"I mean," said Padraich wearily, "that these fortunate orders of ours will have been in the camp since morning. Any officer who chanced to know of their arrival could have seen what was in them, long before that fat fool Dusselman was ever told to find us. That young scoundrel of a captain wanted what you had, that much is certain—and now he has it, and you have nothing in return for it but fair words."

"He's right that it didn't bring good fortune to the man who owned it before me—"

"It would never have come to you, if it had."

"—and I'm not sure it would have helped me, either. I came back safe from Shiloh, true enough, but I think that the better part of good fortune would be to have never taken me near there at all. You saw him touch the blade, Padraich; I think he told me truly what he saw in it."

Padraich gave a scoffing laugh. "Any old woman can look at the palm of your hand and tell you more than that. I'm thinking that the blade was more valuable than you knew, and you've been well and truly cozened out of it."

"That may be so," Kevin said. "Or it may not. The sword's gone now, either way, and we have other things to do."

But he thought all night on Padraich's words, and by morning he was determined to seek out the young captain and have a word of his own with him. His determination was all in vain, however, because Captain Dykes had departed with the rising sun and taken the sword with him, and no one else in camp could recall an officer by that name.

1861
Philadelphia, Pennsylvania

WHEN it came to making certain that the trains of the Philadelphia, Wilmington, and Baltimore Railroad ran smoothly and without interference from the criminal element, Allan Pinkerton was the man in charge. The railroad's problems were his problems, and he had a great deal of latitude in solving them. Over time, he had determined that the most efficient way of solving most problems was to insure that they never had a chance to develop.

That principle had brought him, this January in the Year of Our Lord 1861, to Philadelphia's Mansion House Hotel, which he had chosen for its proximity to the passenger depot at Broad Street and Prime. The railroad had—or would have, in something just over a month—a problem of unprecedented seriousness. On the 11th of February, the president-elect would depart from his home in Springfield, Illinois, for Washington and his inauguration, a journey which would require him to change trains, and train stations, in the city of Baltimore.

Although it lay to the north of the nation's capital, Maryland was in sentiment more closely allied to the slaveholding states of the South. Pinkerton had already begun to hear disturbing rumors, whispers that men—some of them highly placed in Baltimore society—were hatching plans to do Mr. Lincoln harm as he passed through their city.

There's no help for it, Pinkerton thought. *I'm going to have to relocate to Baltimore if I want to have a hope of detecting these traitors.*

It wouldn't be easy, either. Barring great good luck on his part and criminal carelessness on theirs, the only way he would be able to get details of the plot—or plots; it wouldn't do to assume only a single group of conspirators with the will to go beyond wild talk and tavern fantasies—would be to send detectives to infiltrate the plotters. And for a city where the members of society's upper ranks had all known each other since toddlerhood, a month was precious little time in which to accomplish that feat.

The prospect of so much hard work leading only to ignominious failure sat heavily in his stomach, making his contemplation of the Mansion House's bill of fare a joyless thing. On another day, its mock-turtle soup and lobster patties might have tempted him; today he would order plain boiled beef and potatoes and hope to find them more digestible than his thoughts.

"You're thinking about the Baltimore problem."

Pinkerton looked up and saw a man somewhere in that indefinite span of years between middle and old age, clean shaven and with close-cropped hair. The man took the empty chair at Pinkerton's table without waiting for an invitation and added, "It's possible that I can help you with that."

"Do I know you from somewhere?" Pinkerton asked curiously. Even in his lowest moods, the desire to find out and know what was hidden was strong in him, and he could see already that the man now sitting across from him was hiding more things than just a few.

"No, I don't think so," said the stranger. "At least, not yet."

You were telling yourself just now that you couldn't handle this business without a stroke of good luck, Pinkerton thought. *Maybe someone was listening.*

He'd worked with informants before, and knew the risks involved. The ones who offered their services voluntarily were more dependable, in some ways, than those who were bought or coerced into service; but they almost always had reasons and goals of their own that they weren't telling you about, and you could only really trust them as long as what they wanted and what you wanted didn't get in each other's way.

He wondered what this one's private purpose was.

"Tell me more," he said. "Mister—"

"Call me Thomas," said the stranger. "Let's say that I have a gift, Mr. Pinkerton. Like some have the touch, and others have the eye—you have a bit of that gift yourself, if I'm not mistaken—"

Pinkerton didn't bother to deny it. Knowing where to look, and at whom, was a useful knack to have in his business, and if that knowledge alone could have brought in the Baltimore plotters, he would have dined well tonight and rested easy afterward. But a deliberate resistance to detection was harder to penetrate, and there would be those inside the conspiracy who had countervailing gifts of their own. "What use do you believe your gift can be to me?"

"I can see possibilities," said Thomas. "Different futures that may come to pass. Or maybe that *will* come to pass, only not for us here—I'm not a scholar, so I can't tell you the answer to those questions."

Pinkerton said, "Go on."

"I've seen three ways how this Baltimore affair of yours can go, and only one of them is the right way. Ways I've seen include Mr. Lincoln being assassinated in Baltimore, Mr. Lincoln being assassinated in Washington, and Mr. Lincoln not being assassinated at all. 'Assassinated in Baltimore' is a wrong way."

"And which one of them is the right way? I would prefer 'not being assassinated at all.'"

"I can't tell if that's the right way," said Thomas—though Pinkerton's eye told him that the man might know more than he let on. "But Baltimore is a wrong one for sure."

"Mr. Thomas," Pinkerton said, "I am greatly suspicious of the entire state of Maryland, and of the city of Baltimore in particular, but I have no certain knowledge. If I had evidence that Mr. Lincoln would listen to, I could lay it before him and convince him to take appropriate precautions. But if a plot is well advanced, penetrating any secret societies or conspiracies will be very difficult in the small time remaining before the inauguration."

"That's where I can help you," said Thomas.

"You'll have my profound gratitude if you do."

Thomas regarded Pinkerton with what looked for all the world like satisfaction. "That's good," he said. "But first things first—is there any word or phrase that someone could have spoken to you, ten years ago, that would have gained your instant trust?"

Pinkerton thought for a moment. "No. Nor do I think that there is such a word or phrase today."

"That's too bad," said Thomas. "But not surprising. Whom do you suspect to be among the plotters?"

"Citizens of the first rank in Baltimore, extending even to the commissioner of police and the mayor's son."

"That does make things harder," Thomas said. "I know that you have men working for you who are capable of impersonating anti-abolitionists and fire-eating secessionists. But can you lay your hands on a couple who are fit to be introduced into high society?"

"I can," Pinkerton said, thinking of Tim Webster and the Frenchman, who were both already hot to assist him in the Baltimore matter, and needed only to be unleashed on their quarry.

"Good. The next time we meet, I'll have introductions for them."

The man sounded confident of success. Pinkerton looked at him curiously. "Care to explain how you'll be doing that?"

Thomas smiled. "I have more gifts than just one." He pushed back his chair and stood. "Until tomorrow, then. Same time and place?"

"Suits me," Pinkerton said. He must have glanced away for a moment then, because when he turned his gaze once again toward Thomas, the man had already departed.

The next evening, Pinkerton was dining on the Mansion House's excellent chicken fricassee and biscuits when Mr. Thomas joined him at the table. The man produced a folded slip of paper from inside his coat and slid it across the white linen tablecloth toward Pinkerton.

"Have your chosen men meet me tomorrow at this

place, and I'll introduce them to the folks they need to know."

Pinkerton regarded the slip of paper for a moment without picking it up, then turned his level gaze on Thomas. "I spent last night looking over and reorganizing my railroad reports from Baltimore," he said. "And I noticed that they mentioned, from time to time, a gentleman who was deep in the councils of the most violent secret societies and militias, the very ones we are most concerned with. And this gentleman, by all accounts, exactly resembled you."

"I'd call that handy," Thomas said.

"Extremely," said Pinkerton. "I mistrust such handiness."

"You're a suspicious man, Mr. Pinkerton."

"I find that it helps me in my work," he said. "But here is another disturbing thing: I pride myself on my memory. You say yourself that I have the eye; I say that no small part of that gift is that what I have seen, I can recall to mind without gap or flaw. I have read all of those reports at least once before, and I can state confidently that at the time of my first reading they contained no mention of the gentleman in question."

"Most folks would figure that they'd missed it the first time."

"Mr. Thomas, I am not most people."

"I reckon that's true." Thomas leaned back in his chair. "Let me tell you a story, Mr. Pinkerton, and you can judge for yourself whether it eases your mind a little."

"Go on."

"The story begins like this: Once upon a time, about two years ago in fact, there was a man from Missouri who traveled to Baltimore on business. He came from a good family—landowners and magistrates and men of property—and the money he brought with him he spent freely. He was well educated, quoting the classics, and of a quick wit and pleasant demeanor that rapidly drew the trust of men and the admiration of ladies."

"A veritable paladin, in short," said Pinkerton, with a certain amount of cynicism. It had not escaped his notice that the inscrutable Mr. Thomas was also, from his accent, a Missouri man.

"He wouldn't have said so," Thomas replied. "But he took pains to be polite and liberal in his hospitality, though it was observed that he always spoke disdainfully of the abolitionists. He came and went frequently, so that he did not remain long in town and sometimes vanished for months, but his conduct while in Baltimore was always such that he became known over time as a man of calm reserve and good judgment. So it was that when the elections of 1860 came about, some of the leading citizens of Baltimore approached him, as he sat in Cockey's Tavern, to 'sound him out' as to how far he and others like him in Missouri might go in their support of States' Rights. 'If that baboon Lincoln gets elected,' he said to them then, 'that tears it. He'd be a catastrophe.' Which was no worse than what any other man might have said in a hot election year, but then he made some further remarks to the effect that Brutus had been a hero of Rome, for he attempted to stop tyranny by the ultimate act of sacrifice."

"I begin to see where this story is headed," Pinkerton said. "You're going to tell me that they clapped this man on the back and bought him a drink and proclaimed him a stalwart fellow and an uncompromising patriot; and that when he shows up again from Missouri with one or more like-minded young men in his company, his hotheaded Baltimorean friends will accept them without question."

"You're right," said Thomas. "That's just about exactly how it went."

"And you," said Pinkerton, "are almost certainly something other than what you seem. How, precisely, did you accomplish this"—he searched for a word—"this feat of temporal legerdemain? And why?"

"As for your first question . . . I told you, I have more than one gift. And as for the second"—Thomas shrugged his heavy shoulders, and for a moment Pinkerton thought that he looked fatigued—"do you recall that when we met yesterday I asked if there were any word I could give you that would cause you instantly to trust me?"

"I do. And I said that there was not."

"Then I can't say anything else right now, except to ask you to trust me anyway. I'm no abolitionist, but I've gone a long way to preserve the Union. Use me or not, it's your choice—just remember, there's a man's life riding on it, and a lot more than that."

Pinkerton looked again at the folded slip of paper Thomas had laid on the table at the beginning of their conversation, then back at Thomas himself. The gift of the eye was not one that he cared to base decisions on—he preferred solid evidence, of the kind that would satisfy a client or stand up in a court of law—but this time he had no other choice. Thomas bore up under his regard without flinching.

"You are a violent and bloody man, Mr. Thomas," Pinkerton said slowly, "and I am not surprised that the fire-eaters of Baltimore took you to their hearts. But I judge that you are in this matter an honest man, which I will own surprises me, and I am grateful for your offer of assistance." He picked up the slip of paper and tucked it into his coat pocket. "If there is anything you require by way of compensation—"

"Just keep Mr. Lincoln from getting himself killed on his way through Baltimore," said Thomas, "and that'll be enough."

1861

Washington, District of Columbia

THE new president was not a man who could read portents in the motion of clouds or the flight of birds. That was Mary's gift—if gift it could be called, when the weight of it oppressed her soul beyond what a woman should be expected to bear. He'd married her in part for that gift, when he was a young and ambitious lawyer back in Springfield, Illinois, and he regretted that ambition now for her sake.

But she could not help seeing what she saw, and he—knowing *that* she saw—could not stop himself from asking, not in these times, with the Union itself groaning under the strain of the opposing forces at work within it. Even now, on the very night of his inaugural, he had received word that Fort Sumter, under siege in Charleston Harbor, was growing dangerously low on supplies, and must soon either be reinforced or surrender to the forces of the growing rebellion.

Rebellion it would be, and bloody war, if he chose to close tight his grip on the sands that tried to run out from between his fingers. South Carolina was gone already, fleeing the Union at the first word of his election, with Mississippi speeding after, and one by one and two by two the remaining Southern states were falling away: Florida and Alabama, Georgia and Louisiana; even Texas, despite Governor Sam Houston's opposition; and others would follow.

"If the Union does break apart, what shall we do then?"

He'd put the question to Mary, on the last occasion when they were alone together before the start of the inaugural festivities. Her eyes had clouded over, and she had begun to weep.

"Sorrow," she'd said. "Sorrow and mourning and the death of many mothers' sons."

He wanted to know more—was it his action or his inaction that would bring down that great sorrow upon the land?—but he knew from experience that pressing her further would only increase her agitation without adding to his knowledge.

"Rest for a while, Mary," he'd told her instead. "There will be dancing later, and you don't want the Washington ladies to gossip that your eyes were red."

Dancing there was indeed, and lively music, and the ladies in their wide-spread hoops like night-blooming flowers, all in a grand pavilion thrown up a-purpose for the occasion behind the City Hall. He wore white kid gloves, and felt foolish in them, not being a man constructed by nature to be suited for such things; Mary danced a quadrille with Senator Douglas, once a suitor of hers in Illinois. She had said aloud in those long-ago days that whatever man she chose to marry would someday be president, and no one could tell whether it was her vanity talking or the sight that came upon her sometimes whether she wished it or not.

Then, between a waltz and a polka, the thing happened.

The lamps in the pavilion all went dim at once, without so much as a flicker to announce their intention, and an absolute silence muffled everything. The orchestra, taken by surprise, played on for a few notes longer—the conductor's baton cutting the air as he gave the beat, the bows of the violin section rising and falling in silent unison—and then stopped. A diplomat's wife, resplendent in sapphires and a gown of figured silk, opened her mouth wide preparatory to what might have been an impressive display of hysterics, then seemed to collapse in upon herself in silence when her voice failed to respond.

Another moment, and the crowd of guests might have broken apart and fled in wild disorder; but something else happened instead. At the back of the pavilion, nearest to the entrance, a circle of white light began to form out of the shadows. Larger and stronger it grew, until it had attained almost the diameter and shape of a cartwheel and the brightness of a full moon on a clear, cold night. The air around it shivered and vibrated, disturbing the ear with something that was not, or was not solely, music—for certainly, no mortal instruments had ever brought forth harmonies so sweet and so terrible.

Carried on that wave of unearthly music, the great wheel of light traversed the length of the ballroom with slow majesty, not halting until it came to hover above the head of the president himself. Then, as unexpectedly as it had come, it vanished.

The music ended, and the light in the room returned to its normal level. Amidst the babble of voices that instantly arose, the president heard the senator at his elbow exclaiming, in half-hushed tones, "My God, Mr. President! What was that?"

"The newspapers will call it part of the entertainment," he replied, just as quietly. "The ones that don't call it a bad omen of some kind, that is."

"That was no mere entertainment, Mr. President."

"I know. But exactly how much I *don't* know is none of the newspapers' business, and I reckon I'd like to keep it that way for a while."

The senator nodded. "If any man with a notepad and a pencil asks me what I saw, I'll tell him it was part of the inaugural illumination."

"You do that, Senator," he said. "In the meantime, I'll study on what it might have been."

1861

Washington, District of Columbia

THE new president had left the inaugural ball as soon after the mysterious display of lights as possible, pleading exhaustion and the need to ponder the latest bad news from Fort Sumter. Mary had remained behind, blossoming as always in society and the regard of others—and making certain, in her role as gracious hostess, that the peculiar light and its attendant music would not be the only aspects of the ball reported on by the newspapermen.

Now, alone in his office and on the edge of sleep, the president wrestled with the problem still. After a while he became aware that the door from the hall had opened and a stranger had entered, crossing the room to stand in the corner farthest from the windows.

His first thought was that the other was an intruder, a man of flesh and blood come to do him ill. He drew breath to raise an alarm, but two things stopped him. First was the fact that he had not heard the man make his entry, and so presumably neither had anyone else in this wing of the White House. Such silence argued for either a very high level of skill at the stealthier arts, or for an even higher level of skill in other, and more esoteric, disciplines.

Second, the stranger did not appear to offer him any threat. He was unarmed, and from what the president could see of his form and features, he was no longer young. He looked to have been strong and muscular at one time—the president was no stranger to the ways that the hard activity of youth could shape the body of a man when he was old—and even now he held himself like someone used to action, but not intending, at the moment, to act.

"I've seen you before," the president said. "A long time ago, Mr. Thomas, back in Illinois. Why have you come here now, and by what means did you gain entry?"

"I have things I need to say to you," Thomas said. "And I've come through time itself to be here, so you need to listen."

"Signs and wonders are thick in the air tonight already," said the president. "What I need is someone who can read them for me."

"You don't need anything more than your native wit to read the signs tonight," Thomas said. "There's going to be a war, and it's going to be a long and bloody one. Any fool can see that, and nobody with a lick of sense has ever called you a fool."

"'A long and bloody war,'" the president said. He wondered what Mary would say later, when he told her he'd spent his time alone after the ball talking politics with a burglar. "Do you mean the rebellion that's coming?"

"It's the only war I ever knew. I fought for Missouri from 'sixty-one to 'seventy-six; and I'd do it again in a heartbeat if I got the chance, even knowing what I came here to tell you."

"Can you tell me the meaning of what I saw in the ballroom tonight?"

Thomas shook his head. "That wasn't anything of my doing."

"It meant *something*, that's for sure. To make itself manifest on such an occasion, in front of so many, and before me in particular—whatever it was intended to show would have been no small matter."

"Once you find out where it came from," said Thomas, "I reckon you'll know what it is, and once you know what it is, you'll know what needs to be done about it."

"But you can't tell me any of those things."

"You want a seer for that. I'm just a man who's learned a few tricks about walking through time—through the things-that-were, and the things-that-will-be, and the might-have-beens." Thomas's expression darkened. "Sometimes the might-have-beens grow too strong, and drag everything else out of true."

"You're saying that you haven't come here from a fixed and certain future." That was a fair inference, the president thought; as for the rest of the tale, he couldn't tell what conclusion he should draw from it.

"Neither the future nor the past is as fixed and certain as people would like to think," Thomas said. "But some futures are worse than others, and I mean to stop the worst one from being the one that sticks."

"That's a mighty big job."

Thomas shrugged a little. "Where I am now, I don't have much else to occupy my mind."

"How do you propose to go about it?"

"By talking to the man who has the power to act."

"Meaning me, I suppose."

"No other," Thomas agreed. "I'll come back here someday, and when that day comes around, you'll need to do what I tell you."

"What happens," said the president, "if I don't?"

"Ask Mrs. Lincoln," said Thomas. "She already knows."

1861
Springfield, Illinois

THE day's mail included an envelope with a Washington postmark. Mercy recognized the handwriting at once; it was a letter from Mary Todd. The new president's lady was a frequent correspondent, and her letters were perceptive and often witty. The ink on this one was smudged somewhat, as though she had written in haste, or in the grip of some strong emotion.

Mary was often emotional, but Mercy had always thought it best to take those storms of feeling seriously. Her friend could not always explicate the symbolism in which she, herself, dreamed; over time, Mercy had learned that knowing how Mary felt on a particular matter provided valuable clues to interpretation.

Setting the remainder of the mail aside on the table in the front entryway, Mercy took Mary's letter into the drawing room and sat in a chair by the window to read it: quickly at first, her eyes skimming the paragraphs for vital news, then more slowly as she worked to tease out the deeper meanings. The letter began,

My dearest Mercy,
  I have not been in Washington more than a month,

and already I miss your wisdom and your unfailing aid.

I have, of late, suffered repeatedly from the same dream, which I know is a true dream and not merely the disordered fancies of a mind and body worked upon by outside forces. But I don't understand what the dream is telling me.

You are so much more learned than I, and so much more collected in spirit, and moreover you have helped me unravel the meaning of things before. Therefore I have determined once again to lay my burden of dream-images upon your poor uncomplaining back, and beg you to attempt an explanation.

You will have already heard from others about the clever and fantastical illuminations that were part of the entertainment at the Inaugural Ball. I tell you now, Mercy—what we saw in the dancing pavilion was no artifice, though the assembled multitudes—and even the newspapers!—have quite convinced themselves to the contrary. It was, instead, destiny in its purest form, and the burden of obligation that came with it was attached firmly to my husband's shoulders.

I wish I knew what that burden might be. We have known for a long time, he and I—and you also, dearest Mercy!—about the necessity of keeping the Union whole and undissolved, and not allowing "the erring sisters," as Mr. Greeley would have them known, to depart, whether in peace or otherwise. This new obligation is strong, and impressive, and specific—a direct charge to accomplish something—but its exact nature remains unknown.

I feel, however, that coming to an understanding of it is vital to the health of the Republic. Almost every night since that night, I have dreamed of the wheel of ethereal light that descended upon us in the dancing-pavilion. Sometimes there is nothing else in the dream except its presence, hypnotic and all-encompassing, and for as long as the dream lasts I can do nothing more than gaze upon it with wonder and feel myself lapped in its peace. At other times, in other dreams, the light shines ahead of me like a beacon, which I am compelled to seek out through darkness unimaginable, in a forest filled with threats and menaces which I can hear and smell and feel but never see.

Once, and once only, have I dreamed of success in attaining that light. When I reached it, in the dream, and put out my hand to touch it, it began to grow solid and to change its shape. Within moments, it was a sword.

I took the sword into my hand, and felt the things in the dark forest recede, gibbering. But I do not think that the sword is mine; I think that I am only the person charged with passing it on.

I have enclosed a drawing of the sword, just as I saw it in my dream, in the hope that you may have seen it or its like somewhere before. If you should happen to recognize the weapon, I would be pleased to know its history.

Mercy folded the letter and slipped it into the neckline of her gown, where it could rest between her stays and her chemise, close to her skin. The picture of the sword had been roughly drawn—sketching and painting had never been prominent among Mary's skills—but the concentration and memory that had gone into making it had impressed themselves onto the paper along with the strokes of her pen. For the search that Mercy intended to carry out later, it would make a good focus, and keeping it close to her own body would heighten the connection between her and the possibly immaterial thing that the sword represented in the mind of Mary Todd.

With any woman other than Mary, Mercy thought, *I would be moved to regard these dreams as nothing more than a vulgar joke played on a lonely woman by her own unhappy mind . . . a sword that brings her a sensation of peace and happiness when she succeeds in touching it, indeed!*

But Mary is not an ordinary woman. If she dreams of a sword, then it is—or at least was, or can be, or might someday be—a sword. One that her gift of prophecy is increasingly insistent that she find, or cause to be found, or put someone else on the path to finding.

A sibyl's visions of the future, though powerful (powerful enough, Mercy sometimes thought, to pull the present toward them even against its will), could be frustratingly nonspecific, and couched in metaphors not even the dreamer herself could penetrate. For her own part, Mercy had no visionary gifts. She could, if pressed, make cards or crystal or a bowl of India ink show her pretty pictures, magic lantern images of things in the past, or happening afar, or things that by their happening made ripples on the nonphysical plane, but next to a sibyl's sweeping vision, those were merely playthings.

What Mercy's own abilities and training enabled her to do was the thing that Mary could not. She could search for meaning and unravel metaphor, both in the physical world and in the other, and she could, by her gifts, compel mute or recalcitrant things to speak.

She would find the sword from Mary's dream, and she would find what it meant and who was meant to have it. And she would find, most certainly, what the

dark things were that hid in the forest of her friend's
dream, and what kind of menace they presented to
the world.

But a search such as Mercy intended could not be
done lightly. Looking for the physical image of Mary's
dream sword would not—could not—work. She might
leaf through the pages of a thousand dusty tomes, or
visit a hundred collections of arms and armor, without ever finding its match; and that only if she could
gain access to those libraries and those collections.
There were, she thought, entirely too many places in
the world where a respectable matron in a country
at war with itself could not go. Mercy Levering had
never wished to change her physical body for that
of a man—she was quite content with her own—but
the myriad small privileges the world bestowed upon
those who had, by a whim of destiny, been born male
were another matter entirely. Those, from time to
time, she bitterly envied.

With physical searches barred to her, she had no
choice but to fall back upon more esoteric means.
There, she was an expert.

Every day, during the hour that in normal times was
sacred to her midday rest, she searched. Well before
her marriage, while she was still a schoolgirl in braids
and a pinafore, she had claimed that late-afternoon
period for her own—her health, she said firmly, required it, lest she fall prey to nervous collapse. By now,
established as it was by long custom, not a soul in her
household would question what she did (which was,
in fact, what she had always done) during that time.
It was, as it had always been, the hour she kept sacred
for the practice and development of her craft.

Today, as every day, Mercy locked the bedroom

door and drew the curtains. Then she lay supine atop the bedcovers, her hands folded on her bosom, and let her concentration fix itself on the folded piece of paper she carried tucked into her bodice, so close to her heart.

From the lines Mary had drawn on the paper, the sword could have been almost any such weapon. *It would have been too much to ask,* Mercy thought, *for it to have had a distinctive jewel in the pommel, or a runic prophecy inscribed along the blade. She might have described those, even if she could not draw them.* But Mary had seen the sword in her dream, and in her dream the sword had been an object of surpassing beauty and importance. For one with Mercy's talents, that was connection enough.

What she did now was, in its way, an extension of her native gift for influence and compulsion. Somewhere out in the world was the thing or idea or person that haunted her friend's dreams, and she would send forth her thoughts into the aether in order to find it and induce it to reveal itself to her.

Where are you? she asked the darkness behind her closed eyelids. *What are you?*

She let the words roll and echo inside the empty space she had made for them inside her head.

Where are you—what are you—where are you—who are you—where where where where?

It was like walking through a thick mist, over ground with no marked path. Shapes took form in the middle distance, grew larger as she approached, then lost coherence and melted back into the fog. She tried to make them keep solid long enough for her to catalog their identifying features, but it was no good. They would not stay.

Who are you—who are you—Where?

There! One shape held its form long enough for her to begin a rough catalog of its features. *Male. Tall. Clean shaven . . . no. A mustache, cavalry style. Pistols . . . no. A rifle. Or . . . no. Pistols again. A soldier? Or something else?*

The uniform faded in and out. She couldn't tell its color. Maybe it wasn't a uniform at all.

Who are you? What are you? What is your name, your history, your native soil? Who are you—what are you—who?

The figure in the mist sharpened, grew closer and more solid. *Yes!* she thought, with a surge of triumph, and leaped forward, arms outstretched, to seize it and draw it closer—only to have it turn to nothingness in her hands.

She opened her eyes and lay for some time gazing upward at the white-painted ceiling. Sweat beaded her forehead and she drew in air in long, shuddering breaths, as though she had just put herself through some great feat of physical labor. Several minutes passed before she felt herself sufficiently recovered to rise from her bed and sit at her dressing table.

She would restore her appearance—her family would not expect her to wake from her afternoon rest looking as though she had run a footrace—and put off her next attempt until tomorrow. If tomorrow proved equally fruitless, she would try again the day after, and the day after that. She had the scent of her quarry now, and given enough time, she could run it down.

1863
Lawrence, Kansas

IN two years of fighting, first in the Missouri militia and then with Quantrill, Cole had grown accustomed to riding through the hours of darkness
in order to be in the right place for fighting at sunup.
Summer was the time for it, if you had a choice; the
memory of that long night of snow and freezing rain
before the battle of Pea Ridge still had the power to
make him shiver. Better, if you were going to face
hot action come the morning, to have a warm night
under a pale moon, the kind of night where a man
who was sure of himself on horseback could cover the
miles ahead of him in a half-waking, half-dreaming
state, and keep himself rested for what was going to
happen.

Cole agreed with Quantrill's judgment that the
town of Lawrence ought to be hit, and hit hard. Back
in the days before the war, Lawrence had been full of
abolitionists and Free Staters, and it was full now of
Federals and the friends of Federals. Senator and General James H. Lane recruited soldiers for the Union
army out of Lawrence, and it was from Lawrence that
Lane had taken his brigade of Jayhawkers to burn out
Southern sympathizers in the town of Osceola, back in

the year of '61. Now Quantrill aimed to see Lane dead and the burning repaid in full.

He was coolheaded about it, though, and Cole approved of that. A man who had everything planned out and orderly going in was likely to stay calm and take care of his people if things turned bad on the way out. Cole wished he could feel as certain of Quantrill's right-hand man, but he wasn't completely sure yet whether Bill Anderson was just plain crazy or a natural-born son of a bitch.

Cole wouldn't deny that Anderson had a right to make his fight with Lawrence personal. The Federal soldiers who were keeping order in Lawrence might honestly have thought it was a good idea to round up all the Southern-leaning women in town and stick them into a grocery store for safekeeping, and maybe they hadn't weakened the building's structure on purpose when they'd fixed it up to hold so many people, but Bill Anderson's sister Josephine had been killed when the jail collapsed, and his sister Mary crippled. Something like that would make almost any man full of anger and hot for revenge—but Anderson *burned* for it, with a flame that carried more than a whiff of brimstone and the Pit, and Cole wasn't certain he trusted a man who rode with a string of human scalps tied to his bridle.

He trusted Charlie Quantrill, though. Quantrill was a damn sight better at moving men around and getting them to where he wanted them than most of the colonels and generals Cole had known. He'd pulled in bushwhackers and guerrillas from all over Missouri for this raid—some of them had come from so far off that they'd ridden all day to the rendezvous, only to ride again all night. But this would be no straggling, half-organized assault. The day of the attack had been fixed before the call went out, and the hour of it as well—Quantrill's forces, when they hit Lawrence, would do so with a single overwhelming blow.

The raiders came to the top of Hogback Ridge, southwest of Lawrence, in the hour just before dawn. The town was spread out below them, all in darkness on the plain, save for dots of brightness here and there marking where some solitary early-waking soul had risen to do chores by fire or lantern light. The men sat their horses in quiet for the most part, not wanting an alien sound, carried on the early breeze, to alert the townspeople before time.

Cole had brought along four pistols, two holstered and two tucked crosswise into the front of his double-breasted shirt. Most of the raiders had done the same, feeling that it was easier to carry the extra weight of iron than to waste time reloading in the heat of the fight. The sword he'd taken away from the Union corporal in Hannibal, Missouri, made an unfamiliar burden at his left side. He wasn't accustomed to using a weapon like that, but the presence of it brought him an odd sort of reassurance.

He heard a rider coming up beside him, and turned his head to look. It was Quantrill; the dark obscured his features, but the shadowed outline of man and horse together was unmistakable to anyone who'd ridden with him for long.

"Cole," the guerrilla leader said quietly, as soon as he'd come up to talking distance.

"Sir?"

"You're a levelheaded man, and you don't get distracted in a fight."

"Not that I don't appreciate the kind words," Cole

said, "but I have a feeling you're about to ask me to do something."

"You have a suspicious mind. But you're right."

Cole suppressed a sigh. "All right. What do you need me to do?"

"You know that I aim to burn this town," Quantrill said. "And to hang Jim Lane if I can catch him."

"I'd heard," Cole said.

"I've pulled in nearly four hundred men for this—not just our own people, but groups from all over. Most of them can be trusted to deal decently with the womenfolk once the fighting heats up. I want you to keep an eye out for the ones who can't."

"I suppose you want me to stop them before they go too far."

"It would be a good thing."

"May I shoot them?"

"If that's what it takes. But you shouldn't need to do it more than once, so long as you do it in plain sight and make certain everyone knows why. I'll have no insult or violence offered to women, or to children below the age of reason."

"I can do that," Cole said. Then a thought struck him, the memory of young Jake in the jail cell in Hamilton, with the prospect of a hempen noose ahead of him and no beard yet on his chin, and he asked, "What about boy children above the age of reason?"

"If they're old enough to carry a rifle," Quantrill said, "then they're men, and they can die like men."

Quantrill rode away, leaving Cole alone with his musings in the darkness. A few minutes later, the first stirrings of preparation began—the low murmur of orders passed and acknowledged, the restless movement of horses and men, the smell of pitch from fresh-lit torches. If some wakeful soul were to look westward at this moment from Lawrence to Hogback Ridge, Cole thought, they would surely see the flowering of unnatural lights along the horizon and raise an alarm. But no alarm came; anyone stirring on the plain below must be looking eastward, toward the dawn.

The order came to move out. Quantrill was a methodical man. He had a map of Lawrence, and he had loyal townspeople who could tell him which of their neighbors were friendly to the cause and which ones were Federal sympathizers or fire-breathing abolitionists. There were plenty of those in town. Lawrence had been meant from the beginning as a slap in the face to Southerners coming up from Missouri into Kansas Territory, with street names like Massachusetts Avenue and the town itself named after Amos Lawrence of the New England Emigrant Aid Company. The raiders were already divided up into groups—so many houses for each group, no more, with everybody striking at once. Hit fast, hit hard, ride out.

The body of mounted men flowed like water down from the height of Hogback Ridge. Unlike most of those he rode with, Cole didn't carry a torch. That wasn't his part of the work, not when he would need his left hand for the pistol and his right hand for the sword, and a damned good thing that he had a trusted mount under him. As he rode through the darkness, he turned over in his mind the job that he'd been given.

Keep order, Quantrill had said, meaning as much order as could be kept when you were engaged in burning a town and killing all the men of an age to fight back. It wouldn't be easy; Cole would have to deal with men like Bill Anderson, who would stop at nothing when his temper was up. Anderson could be counted on to set a bad example, and others would follow.

Taking on Anderson in person wouldn't be a good idea. Quantrill relied on him too much for that, and wouldn't react kindly to his loss. The man was a bloody-handed maniac but a hard fighter.

One of Anderson's bootlickers, then, Cole thought. *Someone likely to try matching his style. Keep an eye on that one, catch him offending against Quantrill's word. Then take him down hard, in the open where people can see you do it. Make certain they know you'll do it again if you have to.*

Cole had his eye on Gabe Henniker—a close follower of Anderson and always eager to impress his chief. If anybody could be depended upon to go beyond what was commanded and needful, Henniker was the one. As an additional advantage, Henniker was a big man, not easily cowed and unlikely to back down for words alone. Shooting him would probably be necessary, not to mention a positive pleasure and a chance to improve the human race. The only disadvantage Cole could see to the whole idea was that Anderson wasn't going to be happy if someone shot his man, and Anderson, unhappy, could be dangerous.

Cole laughed, low in his throat. *Life* was dangerous these days, and he figured he was up to taking on Anderson if need be.

They were at the outskirts of Lawrence now, and the sky was greying in the east. There was no more time for quiet. Cole heard the command—"Rush on to the town!"—first in one voice, then in many. The raiders broke up into their groups and rode into Lawrence at speed, spreading out through the streets of the town.

Cole had no difficulty attaching himself to Henniker's party. Elsewhere, the first blooms of orange and yellow flared against the grey dawn, and the air that had been so quiet earlier was suddenly full of noises—whoops and yells, shouts of anger and screams of fear, the rattle and bang of gunfire and the high scintillating note of breaking glass. The early-morning breeze carried on it the whiff of smoke and burning.

He saw a house ahead, two stories high with climbing roses on the trellised porch. Whoever built it had been thinking of the future, planting trees in the yard front and back, placed to shade the house in summer once they were fully grown. Not much chance of that now—Henniker called out, "There's our first target, boys!" and the horsemen burst into the yard and surrounded the house like a stream in flood, shooting out the glass in the downstairs windows and setting their torches to the climbing roses, throwing the burning brands into the house through the shattered windows.

"Come on out, you damned Yankees!" Henniker yelled. "We're fixing to burn this place, and we'll burn you up in it if you don't open up and show your faces!"

The door opened. The first out was an old man, then a younger one—of a fit age to be wearing Union blue, Cole thought, if he'd had the guts to volunteer and put his body where his sympathies lay—and finally a woman, barefoot and hastily dressed, with two small children clinging to her skirts.

Henniker raised his pistol. "You know Quantrill's orders," he said, and shot the greybeard in the heart.

More guns spoke, unmuzzled by Henniker's action. The second man went down; the two of them lay in puddles of spreading blood in the dust of their own front walk. The woman wasn't screaming. Cole thought it would be easier for all of them if she had screamed, instead of staring blankly at Henniker with his smoking pistol.

Henniker swung down from his horse and strode up closer to the woman. "Why ain't you crying?" He sounded angry, as if her stunned silence offended him. "A proper wife, she'd be crying to see her man dead in front of her like that. Maybe you need something else to cry for, if you can't cry for him." His hands were working at his belt; Cole tensed, waiting for the moment. "Bill, Matty—hold her down and you can take your own turns with her after."

The woman's eyes had gone wide with fearful understanding. "Please, no. Not in front of my babies—"

Now, thought Cole. He urged his horse forward, shouldered it in between Henniker and the woman, with the pistol level in his left hand.

He pulled the trigger and put a bullet through Henniker's skull without bothering to give him a warning. The man dropped, spraying blood all over Cole's boot and his trouser leg. The woman was screaming now, in gulping, near-hysterical sobs.

Cole ignored her. He had the attention of the whole group, including Bill and Matty, who still held fast to the woman in obedience to Henniker's last order. The Remington New Army pistol in his left hand held five more rounds, and the naked blade in his right hand glittered hungrily in the firelight. Red blood gleamed wetly along its length, though Cole had no memory of striking any man down.

"Drop her," he said.

They obeyed.

"You heard Quantrill's orders. No insult given to women, or to children too young to fight. That's what he said to you. That's what he said to *me*. And I've got his permission to shoot dead any one of you sons of bitches who looks like he's about to forget."

He cast his glance over the crowd of men and saw the one he was looking for—Len Johnson, not as old as most of his companions, and not so hardened—and pointed at him with the steel blade.

"You. Take this woman and her two children to safety in the City Hotel. And if I hear later that you got lost, or that you let them come to harm, then you'll answer to me for it. Do you understand?"

Len nodded.

"Good. Take them and go. And make certain you spread the word that I'll be watching."

He left the dead men and the burning house behind, and rode off toward the sound of nearby fighting. His head was cold and full of echoes, and he hoped he didn't have to do the same thing all over again with the next group of raiders he ran into.

"Still," said a woman's familiar voice, "you made an impression."

He turned his head to look in that direction, and saw one of the straggling not-yet-grown shade trees that now would never protect a house from the summer sun. A woman in a white gown was standing against the grey-brown tree trunk.

"You're not here," he said.

"Not fully," she said, and he recognized the unseen woman who had spoken to him in the darkness by Elkhorn Tavern, and in his dream at the hotel in

Hamilton. "But I've been looking for you for quite a while."

"What do you want?"

"I want your name."

"Thomas Coleman Younger," he said. "Cole. Why?"

But she didn't answer. Instead she turned away and slipped out of sight into the smoke, leaving him alone with the smell of burning roses catching at the back of his throat.

1863

Springfield, Illinois

MERCY Levering Conkling, respected and respectable matron, favored correspondent of the nation's First Lady, sat at her mirror in her home in Illinois. A pair of candles burned on the dressing table, but there was otherwise no light; the curtains of her bedroom were drawn, and the door was locked. The household knew not to disturb her. She had trained them all, even her husband, James, to respect her need for silence and darkness when she pleaded a sick headache and retired to be alone. Her hair was down loose about her shoulders, and her white cotton night robe had neither sash nor buttons, nor binding of any kind. She wore no stays, and her feet were bare. Almost, she could have been dressed for a wedding night, except that hers had long since come and gone—but what she sought to do now required a similar readiness, both actual and symbolic, and a similar willingness to submit to whatever would happen.

"When I was younger," she said, "I studied the arts of persuasion and compulsion. I was quite good at them."

The old man standing in the shadowed corner of

her bedroom said, "I studied on those things a fair bit myself when I was young. But I worked them with smooth talk and pistols, mostly."

She regarded him steadily for several long moments, during which he did not move, and after due consideration found that she had no trouble believing him. His body had the frail appearance of old age, and his face was lined, but something in his carriage and expression told her that in his prime he had been—not handsome, but possessed of the kind of easy attraction that has no problem with making friends or finding lovers. Her mother would have spotted him as trouble in an instant and warned her away from him, not that such a warning would have been needed. Even as a young girl fresh from the schoolroom, with her hair newly put up and her skirts newly let down, Mercy Levering had known better than to trust her affections to a charming scoundrel.

"You weren't born a woman," she said to this one. "Our smooth talk is all reckoned flirtation, and we are taught to carry fans and nosegays, not deadly weapons."

He smiled. "So you found yourself a weapon that no one else could see."

"I've always had it. I just learned how to use it."

"That sort of thing takes time," he said. "And patience. Which I didn't have so much of, when I started out."

"I had an unfair advantage, I suppose. Patience and quietude and a calm demeanor are womanly virtues, and just as long as I practiced all of them conspicuously, nobody cared what else I might be practicing along with them."

He laughed outright this time. "I didn't slow down

enough to get everything in order like that until I wound up in prison."

"Should I be frightened to hear you say that?" she asked. She didn't think that she should; he was not a young man, and she was a cunning-woman of considerable ability. Moreover, she had summoned him here—invited him, if she was being honest, since she knew that, being who and what he was, he had the strength of will to ignore a summons if he chose—and the fact that he had answered her invitation peaceably convinced her that he meant no ill.

"Only if you wanted to sweet-talk me into doing something unwise," he said, and she could tell that he was still amused. "You've got plenty of what it takes to do that to a man."

"Now you seek to flatter me."

He didn't bother to deny it, saying only, "I always did figure that telling the truth was the best way to do such a thing, should it be needful."

It was her turn to laugh, in spite of the gravity of the situation and the seriousness of her plans. "You are a bad man, without a doubt. But you are a bad man with something that I need, and I have"—she paused, considering the right word—"induced you to come here so that I can get it from you."

"You certainly know how to promise a man a good time," he said. "I haven't gotten an invitation like that one since . . . damn, it must have been way back in 1875, down in Florida. But I don't think my joints are up to shenanigans like that anymore."

"Don't worry," she said. "I'm a respectable married woman. What I need from you is something else."

"Too bad. At my age, getting shot at by a jealous husband would be something for a man to brag about."

"I won't lie to you," she said. "What I'm going to ask you for is nearly as dangerous. Giving it to me could kill you."

He didn't look surprised, just curious, and she thought he must have been a daredevil when he was young. "A fair number of things can do that, though a man I trusted told me once that neither steel nor shot nor hemp would kill me. Which particular dangerous thing do you have in mind?"

"You're a time shifter," she said. "You can live in two years at once, in your present and in your past, and you can see any number of possible futures fanned out in front of you like a deck of cards. I want you to teach me how."

"It's not that easy. If you were meant to live two lives at once, you'd already have done it."

"Perhaps."

"No perhaps about it." He frowned. "Why do you want to learn?"

"I have a friend," she said. "A born sibyl. Her gift is a great burden to her, and I'm seeking a way to ease it."

"That's a kind thought, but I don't know as how it could be done. I've heard that whiskey helps, or laudanum for the ladies."

"As long as I have known her, she has dreamed dreams and seen visions . . . but they come when they will and not at her bidding, and she has no sure way to tell a vapor from a warning from a certainty, or any way to tell those things that are merely possible from those things that are foreordained, and that she can do no more to stop or change than any ordinary person."

She paused, looking hard at the old man who stood

in the shadows, who had appeared without noise upon the heels of her most recent summoning, and who would—she hoped—leave her room in the same way when they were done. "But I can do something about them. Only I have to find a way to see them first."

"I don't rightly know," her visitor said, "how I'm supposed to teach you. The man who first taught me—General Albert Pike, that was—all he did was talk nonsense at me for most of a night, then tell me to remember what he'd said and practice everything I'd learned just as soon as I had the time and the quiet for it."

"The long road is always the surest," she said. "But now I find myself in a position where time and quiet are both in limited supply, while the problem at hand is urgent."

"I feel for you, ma'am—I had the same problem myself, for quite some time. But the cure I found isn't one that I'd recommend to a lady. Or to a man either, come to think of it."

"I have in mind something faster and more direct," she said. "But dangerous."

He actually chuckled. He was, she decided, something of a reprobate as well as a daredevil at heart. "I haven't heard a proposition like that in a long time. And never from a respectable married lady like yourself."

"I'm serious. You could end up badly hurt."

"It wouldn't be the first time."

"Still," she said, "I am loath to inflict unnecessary pain or damage. I told you before that I have a certain amount of skill in the arts of persuasion and compulsion. What I think that I can do is persuade and compel the gift locked up in your mind to make itself at home inside of mine."

"If you think that you can do that, I'd be downright pleased to let you. I never asked for any of the gifts I got landed with, and I wouldn't mind getting shed of them before I die."

She rose and extended her hands. "Then let us make the attempt together."

1864
Little Egypt, Illinois

SPYING for Quantrill and for the Confederate army had its dangers as well as its excitements. Wearing a Union uniform and calling himself Captain Dykes meant a ticket to the gallows for Cole if he was caught. Those were the laws of war; and having decided to break them, he was willing to abide the consequences.

The last thing he'd expected, however, was to have his borrowed uniform, and his increasing gift of the touch—he wore his black gloves for a reason now, and not for a subterfuge—mark him out to the civilian populace of a town as someone who could settle their own particular trouble. He couldn't even remember the name of the place that he'd just passed through on his way west, only that it lay in the part of southern Illinois that the rest of the state called Little Egypt. The good citizens there had been suffering from the depredations of bushwhackers and river pirates, and accusations ran high among the factions, each accusing another of passing on information about valuable shipments. With no absolute proof at hand, the arrival in town of an army officer with the toucher's gift struck the city fathers as a blessing direct from heaven.

Hearing their request, Cole had recoiled inwardly in horror. He had no wish to endure a forced handshake with every adult male in wherever the hell it had been. To a man, they were plump, satisfied sorts with no more interest in either side of the war than to make money from it; a moment of involuntary communion with even one of them would have made him queasy, and an entire day's labor at it would likely have left him feeling ill for a week.

He'd promised his hosts that he would, most assuredly, help them make a judgment in their difficulty tomorrow morning, after he'd gotten a good night's sleep. The season, after all, was Christmas, and the good people of the town deserved to enjoy their holiday without holding one another in suspicion any longer.

Then, as soon as it was full dark, he had slipped down the back staircase of his hotel and hit the road again, heading west at first and walking his horse to conserve its strength in case of need. He'd pushed the animal hard for two days already, in a hard season of the year, and in truth his only reason for stopping over in that godforsaken town had been to purchase a few hours of rest for both horse and rider.

He hadn't reckoned on word of his presence in the district reaching the bushwhackers themselves. They were on him before he'd gone more than a mile out of town—a band of rough men, river rats by the look of them, the flatboat men who poled their boats along until they got to landings where the cargo could go onto steamboats. They carried corn, whiskey, and sugar; they carried cotton and tobacco; and they all had lice.

"Touchers," said the center man of the line that stretched across the road in a lopsided semicircle.

He was the biggest and burliest, and stood slightly forward of the rest. "Can't abide 'em. Always putting their fingers on decent people and their noses into other folks' affairs."

Cole thought the complaint a just one, all things considered, which moved him to be temperate in his reply. "I have no quarrel with you, friend," he said, putting his hand near his holstered pistol just in case. "I'm passing through on army business."

"Yah, toucher," another voice said, and a hard shove came against his shoulder blades. The semicircle had shifted to a nearly closed circle while the leader was talking. "Tell us who touched *you*."

"Damnation," said Cole. There were too many in the crowd to shoot them all before he'd need to reload. And even a single shooting would bring down questions that he couldn't answer—particularly when no one in the regiment whose insignia he currently wore would recognize him.

"Couldn't tell who his father is," said another man. They were blocking the road before and behind him now, and getting uglier by the minute. Some of them had lanterns, and the yellow light gave their faces a demonic cast.

A rock came out of the darkness and struck Cole's shoulder. It stung. "The hell with all this," he said. He swung up into the saddle and drew his sword, the one with the bloodstains on it that no polishing could remove. "Try it now, you bastards."

Someone did. A boat pole smashed down onto his wrist, and the sword dropped from his grip. Cursing, he put spurs to his horse's flanks and used the beast's greater mass to smash through the crowd and make his escape, leaving the sword on the ground behind him.

1864
Little Egypt, Illinois

As far as Kevin Mulcahey and Padraich Conner were concerned, life was good. Being sergeants at Fort Butler, the recruitment and training camp for the Illinois regiments, was a posting that most would envy: regular meals, a clean and orderly encampment, and no need either to shoot at the rebels or get shot at by them in turn. And they had fought together at Shiloh, when General Sherman kept the rebels from driving the Union regiments into the river on the first day, and General Grant brought the army back from the dead on the second day and sent the rebels running, so nobody could say that Kevin and Padraich had shirked their duty, or that they were teaching something they'd never known.

Life wasn't all about instructing new recruits in the manual of arms and putting the fear of God and His sergeants into them, however. On this cold, moonless night in December 1864, Kevin and Padraich were chasing a pair of deserters down near Cairo, in the south of Illinois. Normally, the army wouldn't have bothered; new troops were always skedaddling, and it wasn't worth the trouble or the expense to chase them very far. But these deserters had taken with them a string of horses and a wagonload of supplies, and the army and the state of Illinois were not happy about the loss. Sergeants Mulcahey and Connor had been sent to find the deserters and bring them back.

"A fine way to spend Christmas," Kevin grumbled. The two of them had been riding all day, with little chance of stopping before midnight, and no luck at all in their search. "Those supplies are on the river already, heading south. And if our men have a grain of sense between them, so are they."

"And so we'll report it when we get back," Padraich replied. "We can tell them how Little Egypt is packed top to bottom with rebel sympathizers standing ready to help a man load cargo onto a flatboat and take it away, and how the only sure answer is to send down a company or more of men with orders to look in every barn and haystack, and not just a pair of sergeants."

"They'll do no such thing, and you know it. The big men in Springfield would scream bloody murder if ever the army tried a trick like that."

"Aye," said Padraich. "But we're only sergeants, and a pair of Irishmen to boot. Nobody above the rank of major is even going to hear our report. But we'll have made it, and that's what will count."

"You're a cynical man, Padraich Connor, make no mistake."

"All thanks to life in the army." Padraich yawned. "How far to the next town, do you think? I'm all but sleeping in the saddle as it is."

"Too far, I'm thinking," said Kevin. "Nothing for it but to soldier on."

They rode in silence then, their hats pulled down and their collars turned up against the winter cold, until almost midnight.

Hoofbeats on the road ahead of them broke the silence—one man, riding fast. Before long, the rider came into view. The dark of the night obscured his features, but the outlines of his hat and coat suggested a uniform, and an officer's uniform at that.

"Not a lone Rebel, this far north," said Kevin quietly to Padraich as the man drew nearer.

Padraich nodded in reply. "One of ours, then. But what is he doing out on the road alone?"

"Secret business, I'll be bound, and not for the ears of mere sergeants. Wait and see."

The rider slowed as he came up. The faint starlight did little to reveal his features to them, or theirs to him. "I need your assistance," he said as soon as he had approached within earshot. He spoke with a Missouri accent, and his voice had a strangely familiar ring in Kevin's ears. "Sergeants, is it?"

"How did you know, sir?" asked Padraich.

"Nobody else sits a horse like an infantry sergeant," the officer said. "I'm Captain Tom Dykes, of the Twenty-fifth Missouri. I was set upon by robbers a mile or so back, and while I succeeded in making my escape, I left a valuable piece of property behind."

"I *thought* I recognized the voice on you," Kevin said, and tendered a belated salute. "Sir."

"Bold robbers they have in these parts," observed Padraich. "To be taking on such a world of trouble by stealing from an officer like yourself."

"I believe them to be engaged in the illegal river trade," Dykes said. "My guess is that they feared I would expose their more respectable associates in the town nearby."

"That's an answer for your report," said Padraich to Kevin. " 'The fugitives escaped with the aid of sympathetic townspeople.' "

"Chasing deserters, I take it?" said Dykes. "Ride back with me, and we'll see if the property I left behind is still there."

They were close enough now that Kevin could see that the officer's scabbard was empty. "That lost property wouldn't have been a sword, would it, sir?"

"It would have been," said Dykes. "I told you back in Hannibal that I would have it from you, and so I did."

"And vanished before morning," Kevin said.

"Haven't you been enjoying the good life since then, though? Small matters of chasing deserters aside." Dykes turned his horse. "We'll see if the ruffians have left anything behind, and maybe you'll find something of use for yourselves in it."

Kevin wasn't best pleased to be following the orders of the man who had taken the sword from him in the first place—but Dykes was an officer, so what could they do but obey? They rode together up the road in silence, disgruntled on Kevin's part and who knew what on the part of Captain Dykes.

"Not much farther," said Dykes. Then his voice sharpened. "What's this?"

Indeed, there was a smell in the air, like roasting meat that had fallen off the spit onto the hot coals, and dark, unmoving forms lay strewn like boulders all up and down the road.

Padraich said, in a chastened voice, "How many of them were there that attacked you, sir?"

"More than six," said Captain Dykes. "Or I would have put my trust in a revolver and not a fast horse."

"There's more than six here."

"So there are," Dykes said. He sounded thoughtful. "I assure you, sergeants, they were all alive when I won free of them." He swung down from his horse. "Wait here, and keep watch."

The captain picked his way on foot through the scattered bodies, bending now and again to look closer and once striking a match and scanning the scene by its flare of yellow light. When the match had burned out, he strode quickly to a point in the field of the dead, stooped, and picked something up from off the ground.

"I knew it. He lost my sword," Kevin said to Padraich under his breath.

"He has it again now," Padraich replied, as the captain slid the sword into its scabbard and began making his way back to them. "And if these lads here in the road were trying to take it from him, do you want to argue?"

Kevin swallowed. "No."

As soon as the captain was close enough, Padraich asked, "What do you think happened here, sir?"

Captain Dykes shook his head. "I don't know," he said. "The only thing I've ever seen like it was one summer back in Missouri when a herd of cattle got hit by a lightning bolt."

"Lightning out of a clear sky in the dead of winter?" said Kevin. "Do you believe that's what happened, sir?"

"I don't know what happened, Sergeant." He mounted his horse. "We'll have to find a farmhouse and wake someone—it's going to take a wagon to carry all of them to the next town."

"It's a cold night," Kevin said. "With respect, sir, help might be nearer where you came from."

Dykes shook his head. "I think not. Too many in that place are in league with the smugglers and river pirates—they might not take kindly to having friends of theirs brought back like this. We'll head west, and stop at the first town or the next farmhouse. Ask for help there."

They rode west, in the direction from which Kevin and Padraich had come. Captain Dykes didn't seem inclined to talk about what had happened, which Kevin decided was a mercy. There was something about the young officer that made him uneasy, and no matter what Padraich might believe, Kevin didn't think it was only that the man had taken that sword away from him in Hannibal without so much as a "please" or a "thank-you," and didn't show any sign of planning to give it back.

They hadn't been riding long, though, before Padraich pointed and said, "I see a light."

Kevin followed the gesture to look in that direction, and saw that there was indeed a dot of yellow light showing. With so little else visible, it was hard to judge the distance, but it didn't look far off.

"We'll go there," said Captain Dykes decisively.

"It's late in the night for good farm people to be up and about," Padraich said. "What if they happen to be your river robbers instead?"

The captain gave a short laugh, though Kevin didn't hear much amusement in it. "Don't worry. I can find that out easily enough before we tell them what's back there on the road."

Kevin remembered, then, that Captain Dykes had worn black silk gloves when they first met, and that he had handled the sword like a man with the toucher's gift. If he had the gift, though, it didn't seem to make him happy.

"That would set all our minds at ease, sir," he said to the captain. "And thank you."

They left the road and headed cross-country toward the point of light. Eventually, their path brought them to a narrow lane that ran in the same direction, with wagon ruts in it and trees to either side, and they followed that instead. It took them, eventually, to a low, snug farmhouse with a barn nearby. The light came from an oil lantern burning in one of the front windows.

"Sergeant," Dykes said to Kevin. "Go knock on that door and see who answers."

Kevin dismounted, feeling stiff and sore—the captain had been right about infantry sergeants on horseback, which didn't make Kevin any fonder of him. "Yes, sir. What shall I tell them?"

"Tell whoever answers that we're with the army and require their assistance. That's all."

Kevin went up the porch steps to the door of the farmhouse. Behind him, he heard the sound of a revolver being cocked, and felt an unpleasant exposed sensation in his shoulder blades. He told himself not to be a fool, that Captain Dykes was only taking a necessary precaution in case the door was answered not by a wakeful farmer but by a whole gang of angry ruffians.

All the same, he thought, *I do not like the man.*

He knocked twice on the door, then three times, louder, after scorning himself for plying his fist with too much softness and timidity. On the fifth knock, the door swung open. A man stood in the doorway, backlit by the light from the lamp they had seen shining through the window.

"Come in, come in," he said. "I've been waiting all night for someone to come along; I just didn't know who it would be."

"We're from the army," Kevin said. Behind him, he heard the faint noise of the captain's revolver being uncocked. "And we need your help. The officer there can explain everything."

"There are men dead on the main road, about two hours back," Dykes said. Kevin didn't think he'd dismounted yet, but he didn't turn to look. "We need a wagon to fetch the bodies in to town."

"I have a wagon," the man said. "And a pair of mules to pull it, but they're not inclined to work for anyone but me. Tomorrow after the sun is up, I'll take them out."

"Now would be better," said Dykes.

"I have a bad leg," said the man. "A cold winter's night like this one would stiffen it up so I couldn't walk for a week. You gentlemen can put your horses up in my barn and rest here until morning."

"I suppose there's no help for it," Dykes said, but Kevin didn't think the idea pleased him very much.

The three of them put their horses up in the farmer's barn, as they had been invited. "At least they'll get some rest," the captain said, "even if we don't sleep easy."

They went back to the house, and the farmer let them in and led the way into the kitchen, where the oil lamp stood in the window. As he'd said, he had a bad leg, and walked with a pronounced limp. It wasn't until he stood fully inside the circle illuminated by the lamp, however, that Kevin saw his ginger-colored beard and recognized him as the injured man from whom he and Padraich had taken the loaf of bread when they were foraging.

He thought of speaking a warning to the captain, but the words stuck in his throat. He remembered Shiloh, and Mr. Thomas, who had taken him and Padraich out of the swarm of bullets at the price of a promise. A glance over toward Padraich told him that his friend had seen it, too.

It's doomed we are now, for sure, he thought.

He half expected the farmer to accuse him at once, and throw all of them out of his house into the night—*and won't* that *make the captain angry?*—but nothing of the sort happened. Instead, he saw that the man was regarding Captain Dykes with a curious expression.

"Are you a Freemason, Captain?" he asked.

"Something of a nonpracticing one, I'm afraid," said the captain. For the first time since Kevin and Padraich had met him on the road, he sounded pleased with developments. "But if you're willing to take the three of us in for the night for the sake of brotherhood and fellowship, that's all to the good."

"I'll do that," the farmer said; and he was as good as his word, with a bed in the spare room for the captain, and pallets and blankets in the downstairs parlor for Kevin and Padraich.

But Kevin's conscience, and the memory of Thomas's words at Shiloh, ate at him and kept him from sleep. And it was no help at all that the lamp in the kitchen was still burning, and Kevin had not heard the farmer himself go upstairs to bed.

"He'll be sitting in the kitchen," Kevin muttered to

Padraich. "Waiting for us to go to sleep. We should have said we'd sleep in the barn with the horses."

"He never opened his eyes, the whole time before," Padraich said. "He didn't see us."

But still Kevin could not sleep. Finally he stood up from his pallet and said, "There's nothing else to do but confess our sins and ask forgiveness." He took a loaf of army bread from his duffel.

"You've gone mad," said Padraich with conviction, but he rose and followed Kevin into the kitchen just the same.

The farmer was sitting at the kitchen table waiting for them. "I thought that you two would come back for a talk," he said. "Sit awhile."

They took seats at the table. Kevin placed the loaf on the tabletop, pushed it across, then clasped his hands together on the tabletop and said, "We've met before, when Padraich and I were foragers with the army."

"In Tennessee, before I sold my farm there and came north to be out of the way of the fighting," said the farmer. "Yes, I remember."

"How?" asked Padraich. "You never once opened your eyes while we were there."

"Nevertheless, I am a man who sees things," the farmer said. "As I see a great deal that is interesting about you, and not the least of it has to do with that fine sword your captain carries with him."

"He's not our captain," said Kevin. "We only met him tonight on the road."

The farmer nodded and looked pleased. "Then you won't mind taking that sword back from him while he sleeps, and being on your way."

"Tonight?" said Padraich. He sounded disappointed.

"You have to take the sword to Washington, and give it to President Lincoln, don't you?" The farmer looked from one to the other of them and smiled above his ginger beard. "I told you I was a man who saw things. One of the things I saw was the promise you made at Shiloh; and now that I've seen you mean to keep the first part of it, I'm bound to help you keep the second. Take the sword, and the wagon and the mules, and be off with you before daybreak."

"I thought you told Captain Dykes that the mules wouldn't work for anyone but you," said Padraich.

"I said that they're not *inclined* to, which is true enough, they being mules. I could just as truthfully have said that I wasn't inclined to work them—but sometimes a man will forgive in a mule what he won't take from a fellow human being. An odd thing, but there you are."

"What if the captain wakes when I go to fetch the sword?" Kevin asked.

"He won't," said the farmer. "I can see that, as well. He's ridden longer and harder than either of you for two days already, and now he sleeps like the dead. But the first light will wake him, so you need to hurry and be on your way."

1864
Little Egypt, Illinois

C OLE woke up as the first light of morning came
in through the window. He'd slept well—
better than he would have if he'd stayed back
in the town, even with the problem of what to do
with the dead men back on the road still needing to
be taken care of. Meeting up with the two Federal
sergeants had almost thrown him, but he'd been fortunate there, as well. The more suspicious of the two
had been so taken up with resentment over the loss
of his undoubtedly looted sword that he hadn't had
attention to spare for anything else; then they'd found
the dead men in the road.

*Lightning that no one saw, out of a cloudless sky, on a
cold, moonless night.*

Cole shivered under the farmer's quilts and blankets.

He'd have to go back there today, with the man and
his wagon, if he wanted to keep up his disguise and
stay out of trouble. But he'd need to work fast if he
didn't want to lose any more time on his way out to
take care of the Confederacy's business on the coast.
Crossing the mountains would be troublesome this
time of year; he'd have to turn south as soon as he

could. Out in the far west, the army was mostly about chasing off the Indians, and he could change his borrowed uniform for regular clothing and be plain Mr. Dykes, on the road to Oregon by way of California.

Get up, get it done, and get moving, he told himself, and threw off the blankets before he could lose his resolution.

The cold in the room hit him like a slap with a board, and he was halfway into the Federal uniform and working on the gold buttons before he saw that the sword and its sword belt were no longer hanging from the bedpost where he had left them.

"God *damn,*" he said. "I trusted that redheaded son of a bitch. That'll teach me to put any stock in Masonic oaths and signals and suchlike tomfoolery."

"Your revolver is still here," said a familiar voice. It was Mr. Thomas, sitting in the rocking chair by the window and looking amused. "And your money. And there's nobody waiting downstairs to arrest you for being a rebel spy."

"Then why did he take my sword?" Cole demanded.

"He didn't. Your friend Sergeant Mulcahey did, and is long gone with it."

"Stealing from an officer! I'll have him—" Cole stopped and took a deep breath. "I'll remember that I have more important things to do than chase a pair of thieving Irishmen, and Yankee Irishmen at that. If Sergeant Mulcahey wants that sword so much, he can keep it."

And if it doesn't concern him that the last pack of thieves who had it are lying dead on the road, then it doesn't concern me, either.

"I don't believe he'll be keeping it for long," said

Thomas. "But that's no longer your problem. If I were you, I'd thank Mr. Dunning for his hospitality and head west without asking any more questions."

Cole sighed. "You're not me. But I think you're right."

FLORIDA was a pleasant place, or at least Cole Younger found it so—hotter and stickier than Missouri, but greener, and the frequent rains kept down the dust. The state's tough little piney woods cattle had fed the Confederate army sufficiently if not well for years during the war, and now also fed beef to the island of Cuba. Rounding up the cattle and driving them overland to Punta Rassa for shipment to Cuba by boat was sweaty, sometimes dangerous work, but the Cubans paid for their beef in gold, not paper. An experienced cattle drover could make good money off his part of the trade, and Cole had experience. He'd worked with livestock since before he was old enough to call himself a man, and next to raiding and soldiering, it was the occupation that he knew best.

The cattle trade had put enough money in his pockets to let him do right by the older of his two brothers, sending him off to Virginia to study law at the College of William and Mary. Jim Younger was the quiet sort, four years Cole's junior and fond of books and music, and with a good solid education behind him there was no telling how far he might go—he might become a lawyer or a judge, or even go into politics. Albert Pike was on his way to the Confederate Supreme Court, after all, and once he was settled in Richmond, perhaps he might be willing to lend a hand to the brother of an old comrade.

Cole had put his brother on the northbound train from Lake City just that morning. Now he was heading back to his rooming house full of the satisfaction that comes of a job well done. As he approached the house—a big, white-painted building set up off the ground on pilings after the local style, with a deep, shady verandah running around three sides of it and a dogtrot leading to the kitchen in the back—he perceived a woman sitting on the porch swing.

She wasn't one of the regular boarders at the rooming house, he saw that at once. He would not have forgotten someone with her good looks. She wasn't pretty like a painting on china or a drawing in a ladies' magazine, all ringlets and dimples, but she was striking, with sleek dark hair and the sort of good bones that would last far longer than dimples would. She had a pitcher full of lemonade sitting on a table next to the swing, and she was sipping at a glass of it through a straw.

Cole tipped his hat as he passed her on his way to the front door; she stood and addressed him.

"Coleman Younger?"

He'd made no secret of his name while he was doing business here in Florida. There were enough shady fellows in the cattle business that it made more sense to let himself be known as a reliable man from a good family. He nodded at the woman and said, "Yes, ma'am. Can I be of service to you?"

She smiled, sweetly, but modestly, too.

"Oh, Mr. Younger," she said. "Yes, sir, you may."

Cole said nothing, waiting for her to continue. He kept his hat in his hand. The day was pleasantly warm, without the humidity that would come with the late-afternoon rains, and he was in no hurry to go into the house, or, indeed, to go anywhere. At length, when she did not explain herself further but continued to smile at him in a friendly manner, he said, "Ma'am, I'm afraid you have the advantage of me. Whom do I have the honor of addressing?"

He feared at first that she might chastise him for speaking to her so boldly without an introduction, but she did not—which was fair enough, he thought, since she had already called out to him by name, and in public, too.

"Does my name make a difference?" she asked, whispering, perhaps to herself. Then she spoke to him directly. "My name is Mercy. And I believe that you've been expecting me, sir. An associate of Grandmaster Pike—whom I believe you know—told me that I should seek you out, because I know something that you'll need to learn."

"Grandmaster Pike?" Cole furrowed his brow. "I fought alongside a *General* Pike in the course of the late unpleasantness, and he's on the way to being Mr. Justice Pike these days."

"I think he may once have been a general," Mercy said. "There were so many of them, after all."

"There surely were," Cole said. And Albert Pike, he reflected, had been one of the strangest of them. Pretty as the woman who called herself Mercy was, the fact that she admitted to having been directed to him by one of General Pike's associates inclined Cole to think that she was not necessarily everything that she seemed to be. It occurred to him that while he had seen her take the glass of lemonade in her hand, and had seen her appear to drink from it, he had not actually seen her swallow. She had a very fair, white neck, and the action would have been difficult to hide.

Well, then. His wartime acquaintance with General Pike and Mr. Thomas had left him with one or two small knacks of his own. He pulled off his black silk gloves and tucked them into his coat pocket, then gave a half bow and extended his arm.

"Ma'am," he said. "May I invite you in?"

"Oh, no, sir," she said, drawing back. "That wouldn't be proper. We hardly know each other. Yet."

"Then let me refresh your glass for you," he said, nodding toward the pitcher of lemonade. "The day may turn sultry."

She smiled at him, and her eyes were bright and knowing. "Why, thank you, sir," she said, and held out the half-empty glass.

He took it from her, their fingers touching briefly, then added more lemonade from the pitcher and gave it back. Her smile became, if possible, even more knowing than before, and he knew that she understood what he had done, and why. She had let him do it anyway, which meant . . . something, but he wasn't yet sure exactly what. He sat down beside her on the porch swing and smiled back at her in return.

"Now," he said, "what is it you want to tell me?"

"What you've suspected ever since the war," she said. "You already know that it's possible for a person to work themselves free of time and space and move about from year to year just as easily as other men might cross the street. And since you've made a point of touching my hand, Mr. Younger, you have to know that at this moment I'm doing that very thing."

Memory—*a lantern-lit clearing in a dark wood, the old man and the general pronouncing dire oaths and making obscure promises, the unwelcome advent thereafter of his toucher's gift*—came at last to his aid. "Then you're the messenger that General Pike and Mr. Thomas said would come to me when I needed him?"

"I am."

"Took you long enough," he said. "Ma'am."

"I had to learn how to get here first," she told him. "And the learning wasn't easy, either."

"Was that the only thing you came here to tell me— that you *could* come here to tell me?"

"No," she said. "There are other things."

"Go on."

She looked at him squarely then, all traces of light amusement gone from her face. "The first thing that you must know is that this permanent division between the states is a deadly one. You and your family stood for Missouri and for the Union until it was no longer possible to favor both, and then you chose Missouri and disunion. *But you made the wrong choice.* This Southern Confederacy of yours will wither and collapse without the support of its abandoned sisters— and given enough time, the same things will happen to the North. As harsh as war always is, the future will be worse for everyone if the Union is broken permanently."

The declaration put his back up. He'd given years of his life and a good part of his family's fortunes to the cause of Southern independence, and hearing it dismissed as flat-out harmful rankled, even from the lips of a pretty woman. "You know all that for certain, do you?"

"I have it from the mouth of a sibyl," she said flatly.

"Not a card reader or a stargazer or a caster of bones, but a true prophetess. And I promised her that I would do all in my power to stop it. So I need you to make sure that the North wins the war."

"Ma'am," Cole said, "that's a tall order. I fought against the North, and I helped make damn sure that they *lost* the war."

"It's not too late to change that."

"You're asking me to turn traitor."

"Not at all," she said. "I'm asking you to save the world, or at least all the parts of the world that my friend can see."

"That sounds like a hard job, even if I was inclined to do it. Which I can't honestly say that I am."

"You won't need to lift a hand against any of your own, or to betray a single trust."

Cole regarded her thoughtfully. "I'm a cattle drover," he said, "and my name isn't one for the history books. I doubt that there are ten men among my old companions who recall it now. I think you and Mr. Thomas and General Pike have picked the wrong man."

"Nothing is fixed and certain," Mercy said. "You only need to do one thing: Find the sword of the Butlers and deliver it to Abraham Lincoln."

"Mr. Lincoln finished his term in 1868 and moved back to Illinois, saying that he would never again hold public office," Cole said. He wondered what time she had come from, that she could talk with such certainty about nameless and dreadful futures but not know the common facts of the recent past. "So I wouldn't find him in Washington even if I did have a sword to give to him."

"It's a bit more complicated than just taking a train," Mercy said. "You need to learn the other thing that I have to tell you, which is the secret of moving through space and time. I hope you won't think me too forward, but you've touched my hand already, and learned something of me from that. For complete knowledge," she said, casting her eyes down demurely, "more touching is required. It's a necessary thing . . . though I imagine you won't find it too unpleasant. And I certainly will enjoy the teaching."

"Do you mean—?"

"That's part of why Thomas and Albert didn't want to take you the whole of the way," she said. A blush rose up in her cream-colored cheeks. "Now, how would you like to show me your room?"

"Ma'am," he said, "I'd be delighted."

He had a corner room on the uppermost floor of the boardinghouse—small, and at the top of a long climb, but with windows on two sides that he could open to let the breezes blow through. The bedstead was metal painted over with white enamel, and the coverlet was pieced out of scraps. Yesterday had been laundry day, so the sheets at least were clean. He closed the door and locked it behind them.

A ladderback chair stood next to the bed. Mercy sat down, and bent to unbutton her shoes. She took off first one and then the other, then lifted her skirt to roll down and remove her stockings, laying bare small, high-arched feet and trim ankles. Then she rose and stood barefoot on the wooden floor.

"This is not something that can be done by half measures," she said. "We must both be naked to the touch." She was blushing again, in defiance of the forthrightness of her speech. She didn't look frightened, though, which pleased him; he'd never seen the point of a scared woman.

He said, "Fair enough," and hung first his hat and then his jacket on the wooden peg behind the door before turning his attention to his cuffs and collar. He had removed them and laid them on the dry sink next to the washbasin, before it occurred to him that a cattle drover—even a prosperous one—had an unfair advantage over a woman of fashion when it came to reaching the state of nature.

"You have too many buttons," he said. "Looks to me like you could use some assistance."

"If you would be so kind."

He stepped around behind her and began unfastening the row of tiny buttons that ran down her back from the nape of her neck to below her waist, taking care not to let his fingers touch her bare skin. Skin would touch skin eventually, but he was in no hurry to experience what the touch might reveal. He worked the sleeves down over her arms, and let the dress fall down over her petticoats to the floor, leaving her standing in nothing but her underpinnings.

His mother and sisters, he thought, would have known all the different names for the bits and pieces, would have known all about eyelet lace with ribbon threaded through it, and about what a respectable woman might wear to a meeting that—if he rightly understood Mercy's state of mind—lay somewhere in the middle ground between a seduction and a lodge initiation.

"Your turn," he said, and stood still while she unbuttoned his shirt and then his undershirt, and slid them off his shoulders. She, too, took care not to touch skin against skin, pulling away the garments with slow concentration until he stood bare to the waist.

The breeze coming in through the open windows hit his skin and cooled the summer sweat, raising the hairs on his arms and chest.

"Boots," she said. Her voice had a catch in it that he hadn't expected. "You'll need to take off your boots before you go much further."

"I was distracted," he said, and sat down on the edge of the bed. "I can't imagine why."

He tugged at his right boot. She bent to help him—a matter-of-fact movement, nothing coquettish about it, and one that made him wonder who it was she'd grown accustomed to helping out this way. The eyelet lace on her chemise lay against the tops of her breasts; when she pulled the boot off his foot, the lace shifted with her movement to reveal the upper curve of the crinkled brown skin around each nipple.

His boots and socks removed, she straightened and stepped away again. Her fingers worked on her chemise and corset and petticoat, dropping them one by one to the floor. At the end, she turned partly away, so that when the last garment fell he saw only the curve and flare of her back and her sweetly rounded bottom. She was not by nature as bold as she had nerved herself up to be, he thought.

"Now you," she said. "We have to be equal for this."

He didn't argue.

"All right," he said a minute or two later. His voice cracked; he bit his lip, took in and let out a deep breath, and went on. "I'm ready."

She turned around. He drank in the sight of her— the round white breasts, the hollow of her navel, the dark curling hair of her sex—and thought that if he dared to embrace her he might weep.

"It's been a while," he said. "The touch—gets in the way of things, sometimes."

She moved closer to him, so close that he could see the pulse beating in the curve of her neck, though still there was not yet the contact of flesh against flesh. "Not for this, Thomas Coleman Younger. For *this*, it is necessary."

He reached out and took her hand. Her skin was soft against his calloused fingers, and warm to the touch. He felt her heartbeat, faster than his own but strong and steady, and sensed the deep inhale and exhale of her breath. The secrets of her mind and soul she kept behind strong walls; no casual touch would breach them, and he was grateful.

Then she reached up and put her other hand behind his neck, and drew his mouth down against hers, and a circle that he had not known existed snapped closed and burned into life.

Ouroboros, her mind said in his. *The serpent of eternity, that bites its own tail forever.*

Later, as they lay spent and exhausted on the rumpled sheets, her head upon his arm, Mercy said, "That sword you once had, you'll have to find it and fetch it."

"And give it to Mr. Lincoln?" he asked her drowsily.

"Yes," she said.

"I haven't said yet that I'll take your job."

"When the time comes, you'll know what you have to do. And I've given you the means to do it."

"Should I be grateful?"

"Probably not," she said.

He pressed a kiss against her temple. "It's all right," he said, and drifted off to sleep.

He woke from a slumber full of confused and vaguely erotic dreams to find his room disappointingly empty, though he could not clearly remember why he thought at first that it should have been otherwise. The first drops of a summer afternoon rainstorm were dashing against the windowpane, and his clothes and boots lay in a tumbled pile on the floor.

Now, what the hell did I do?

For a moment the question hung unanswered. Then belated memory awakened, and he recalled playing poker all through the night and into the morning with his brother Bob and a couple of railroad men, then eating a breakfast of steak and eggs before calling at the post office to pick up his mail. There'd been a letter for him from Missouri, addressed to the "Mr. Dykes" that was his name these days in the cattle trade. He didn't think that any of his troubles with the law had followed him down to Florida, but it never hurt a man to be careful, especially when he'd had the misfortune to come out on the losing side of a war.

He'd meant to read the letter as soon as he got up to his room, but he'd been so tired, and so hot and sticky with sweat, that he'd stripped to the buff and fallen asleep on top of the coverlet with the letter still lying unopened next to the washbasin. Groaning, he sat up, snagged the letter, and worked his finger under the flap of the envelope, then pulled out the sheet of paper inside.

The writer was his sister Sally. *Dear Cole,* she wrote, *I hope that this finds you well in Florida. The money you've been sending us has been real helpful, but we need you here. Things have been bad all over Missouri, and not all of our friends know how to get along like you do. I'm always afraid they're going to fall in with bad company and get themselves hurt. They sure could use your steadying hand. Your old friend Frank tries his best, but I don't think he's quite up to it.*

"Well, damn," said Cole to the empty room. "I guess we're going home."

1876
Lee's Summit, Missouri

ABOUT four thirty in the afternoon on a hot, overcast day in early summer, a buggy driven by an old colored man drove up the road leading from Lee's Summit, Missouri, to the home of Cole Younger, cattle drover and reputed bad man. A woman wearing a figured organdy walking dress and a flowered bonnet got out of the back of the buggy and came up alone to the door. There she was greeted by Aunt Suze, the Younger family's cook and maid-of-all-work, who admitted the lady to the front parlor.

Mr. Cole himself shortly came down, wearing a collarless shirt but no coat, for the heat of the afternoon was oppressive and he had not been expecting callers. His Remington revolver he had left behind in the upstairs room where he had been resting, since he did not expect the shooting kind of trouble from a woman arriving alone. The lady who was sitting in the parlor when he arrived, however, was not any of the ones he had thought likely when Aunt Suze roused him from his nap.

But he had known her once; the sight of her brought memory back in a rush, though he had not once thought of her since they had parted. When she smiled at him and said, "I trust you remember me?" he said, "I do now. Your Christian name is Mercy. I never had time to learn the rest of it. We met in Florida, a year or so back."

"Do you recall what we spoke of, and the gift that I gave you then?"

"I know that between the time I lay down with you and the time I got up again, something happened that changed everything," Cole said. "The devil of it is that I can't remember exactly what it was that changed, or exactly what we did that changed it. Are you proposing that we do something like that again?—because I'm flattered, ma'am, if you are, but one set of changes that I can't quite remember is more than enough."

"I don't know what you mean, I'm sure," she said; but the blush that rose to her cheeks belied her claim of innocence. Again she smiled at him straight on. "I could do with some lemonade, though, if it's not too much trouble."

Cole nodded to Aunt Suze, who departed in the direction of the kitchen.

"She'll make a lot of noise returning," Cole said. "She's discreet that way, and she won't spread gossip. Now that she's gone you can tell me truly—what brings you here?"

"I know where the sword of the Butlers is currently resting," she said. "You found it once. You'll want to find it again."

"Say I do," said Cole. "What's riding on it?"

"The fate of the Union."

"Say I don't care."

She looked at him sharply. "Say that you do."

"I'm not promising anything," he said. "Speak your piece."

"It's in a bank vault," she said. "That sword once belonged to the Butler family, and it's gone home to them. Benjamin Butler—"

"The Beast of New Orleans Old Silver Spoons. Yes." Butler's tenure as commander of the Union forces occupying the Crescent City had not gained him any friends in the South—not that Cole had ever heard that he'd gone looking for any. More than one New Orleans lady, it was said, owned a chamber pot with Benjamin Butler's portrait painted inside on the bottom.

"Benjamin Butler is part owner of a bank, and the sword is in the bank vault there." The corners of her mouth turned upward. "For safekeeping, if you'll pardon the term."

Cole regarded her narrowly. Her mouth was still very sweet to look at, but she herself was attractive in the same way that a well-made gun or a fine knife was attractive—you knew just by looking at it that you might be able to do great things with it, but that if you got careless it would kill you dead. "And how do you come to know about the bank and the sword?"

"The same way that I have had to learn everything else about you, Mr. Younger," she told him. "I went places and I saw things."

By traveling between times, he supposed, as she had said in Florida that he would be able to do, and that Mr. Thomas and Albert Pike had told him was possible the night before Pea Ridge. He wondered if she was traveling that way now, or if she had journeyed overland in the normal manner to seek him out. He noticed for the first time that she wore a wedding band—he could not remember whether or not she had worn it that day in Florida—and wondered if her husband knew everything that she was, underneath the respectable manners and the fashionable clothes.

"Where is this bank?" he asked.

"A place called Northfield," she said. "In Minnesota."

"That's a long way from Missouri."

"You've gone farther. Florida and California and other places besides."

"I don't owe you any favors," Cole pointed out.

"I know that," she said. "But you'll study on the question, if I know you. And after all this time, I believe that I do."

Aunt Suze returned then, with—as Cole had predicted—a great deal of noise and stomping, bearing two glasses of lemonade on a tray with a rye-grass straw for each.

Mercy took her lemonade and stood up, still holding the glass in her hand. "I can't stay, I'm afraid. I still have quite a ways to travel."

"I'll see you out," he said. "And please, take the drink with you. The day is sweltering, and a bit of refreshment never goes amiss."

"Thank you," she said. "I'll remember this kindness, the next time we meet."

"And when will that be?" he asked.

She gave him another of her sharp, dangerous smiles. "I think you know."

He looked at the glass. "I expect I do," he said, and held open the door for her, and the door to the buggy, too.

Aunt Suze stepped up beside him as he stood watching the road down which the buggy had disappeared. "I don't like that one," she said. "She's a bad 'un, like that Shirley girl who always used to be coming around."

"I know," Cole said. "What do you think I'd find if I mounted up and followed that buggy?"

"The tracks'd vanish from the dust before you'd gone half a mile, and no sight more. Maybe a smell of sulphur in the air."

"I reckon you're right," Cole said. He drank the lemonade. It was good. Not too sweet. It quenched his thirst. "Listen, I'll be going out later, perhaps. Calling on Frank and Jesse, if anyone else needs to find me."

"You aren't planning on doing anything foolish, are you, Mr. Cole?"

"Only if it's necessary," he said. But he knew already that whatever he ended up doing would be both foolish and necessary anyway. He was feeling the world start to shift beneath his feet again, like the tremblings in the earth he had felt when he journeyed out to California near the end of the war, but he didn't yet know what the change would be.

1876
Minneapolis, Minnesota

THE gang took the train north from Missouri through Iowa to Minnesota. Cole found it odd, rattling over the open grassland in a railroad car on the way to a bank job—*the last one,* he'd said to his brothers, and to Frank and *his* brother; *after this, we split up, take the money and start over someplace else, Cuba or South America maybe*—but he supposed that by now he should be accustomed to a life filled with odd things.

The gift of the touch that he'd picked up, or been stricken with, somewhere between Pea Ridge and Lawrence had never quite gone away. He never spoke of it to his brothers, or to the various men they'd ridden with over the years; if any of them had ever guessed the secret, they didn't speak of it to him, either. He'd taken to wearing gloves most of the time after the war was over, except for work or for fighting, which to strangers was as good a signal as any, but Jim and Bob and Frank and Jesse had known him back when he was plain Cole Younger with no gifts at all. They didn't know that a man born ordinary could be handed gifts he hadn't asked for, with no way to give them back.

Minnesota, when they reached it, turned out to be full of lakes and trees, forests of white pine hiding the horizon and crowding too close to the railroad line for comfort. When this job was over, he thought he might take his share of the money, and Richard Butler's sword, and go away with them to Patagonia. They raised cattle there, and all the descriptions he'd read of it made it sound like a place with plenty of sky.

One thing was for damned sure—he couldn't take the sword and give it to Abraham Lincoln, more than ten years dead and buried in Springfield.

At the end of the railway journey, the group split up as Cole had arranged it: himself and Charley Pitts to scout out the rivers, bridges, and fords between Northfield and the Iowa line, and the others to spread out and purchase horses and supplies. Charley was new to the gang, and Cole still wasn't sure about bringing in somebody from outside their established circle for what was meant to be the last big job, but he'd thought hard about it and couldn't see a way to tackle the Northfield bank with any fewer men. He'd have been even happier if he could have brought along at least one more rider besides Charley Pitts, but dependable men were hard to find.

Some of his thoughts and worries must have eventually worked themselves through to show on his face, because on the last day they spent scouting, Charley asked, "What's the matter, Cap?"

You didn't ride with me in the war, Cole thought; *you don't get to call me by that name.* But he didn't bother protesting. Frank James called him that, and Frank had been Private James when Cole was Captain Younger, and the others in the gang would take their cues from Frank no matter what Cole said.

"I'm just wondering about things," he said. "This place makes me feel strange."

"It's because you're out of Missouri," Charley said. "You'll be all right once you're home."

"The trees here are too close together," Cole said, doing his best to make it sound like a humorous complaint. He wasn't going to spook Charley by voicing his real thoughts aloud. *I felt this way in Florida, when I lay with Mercy and everything changed and I changed too, so that I couldn't tell afterward what had changed and what hadn't.*

"So what are we doing here, if you don't like this place? Why not just ride back south and forget all about it? There's nothing up here anyway but Yankees and squareheads as far as the eye can see."

"There's something yonder," Cole replied, waving his hand vaguely in the direction of Northfield, "bigger than all of us."

"Then we're going to have a damned hard time carrying it all the way back to Lee's Summit."

"So we will," Cole said. "So we will."

They met back up with the rest of the gang in Minneapolis, where they had rooms in the Merchant's Hotel. They'd be living rough on the overland journey back to Missouri, and Cole thought they might as well have some comfort behind them going in. There was a barroom in the hotel, and tables big enough for a friendly game of cards.

Bill Chadwell, an Illinois man and one of the group that had gone to buy food and horses while Cole scouted out the land, said to him, "Care to play a hand or two?"

"Why not?" Cole said, thinking that a round of cards would do more to settle his restless spirit than brooding alone in his room. He pulled off his gloves and put them into his pocket before he sat down at the table. Work and fighting were not the only activities for which gloves were a hindrance.

"You're hot tonight," Bill said after the first few hands. "If your luck with the cards was this good all the time, you'd never need to do a dishonest day's work."

"My luck comes and goes," Cole told him. "Mostly it goes. Just not tonight."

Only it wasn't luck at all, not this time. Tonight the cards were talking to Cole as they never had before. He could feel what the suits and numbers were without looking at their faces, and he could hear them whispering things to him about what the other men held in their hands. The voices of the cards filled his mind and left him feeling like his braincase had been stuffed full of lint. He was simultaneously removed from the events around him, and observing them. He saw things, and knew things, that he couldn't help. And one of the things he knew was that Bill Chadwell—Bill, raking in the silver dollars; Bill, laughing and smoking a Cuban cigar—was playing in his last game. Every time Cole touched a card that Bill had touched, he could feel death.

Then his youngest brother, Bob, came in and sat down at the card table and said, "Deal me in."

Bob had no more than pushed in the ante when his hand brushed against Cole's, and Cole knew that Bob, too, was playing his last game. Bob would die in prison, struggling to draw breath.

"Excuse me, gents," Cole said, and folded.

He stood and walked upstairs to his room before he could be sick to his stomach. The first time he'd ever touched that damned sword, in the tavern in Hannibal where he'd taken it from that thieving Irishman Mulcahey, he'd seen the price that came with owning it, and now he was going to pay it, too. He didn't dare look into the mirror in the room, lest he see the knowledge of it in his face.

"Yes, you've played your last game as well," Thomas said. He was looking older than Cole had ever seen him, and was sitting on the bed.

Cole didn't even bother feeling surprised that he'd shown up. He only said, tiredly, "I die, too?"

"Everyone does," Thomas said. "Eventually."

"You know what I mean."

"I know. But you won't die by steel, lead, or hemp, if that's what you're asking."

"That isn't much of a comfort," Cole said.

"Then console yourself with the knowledge that you're doing what duty and honor both require."

Cole snorted. "Honor. *That* got Missouri a long way."

"Farther than either of us will ever live to know," Thomas said. "But we do what we must."

"What if I say no? I still have free choice, don't I?"

"Yes, you still have free choice. But I've seen pictures of what things will be like if you say no. You wouldn't like it."

"If God's revealed something to you, then you're obliged to believe it," Cole said. "But nothing in heaven or earth says that *I* have to believe *you*."

"Nothing says that," Thomas agreed. "Maybe I'm your guardian angel, or maybe I'm the devil come to lead you astray. You'll have to make up your own mind about that."

He stood and walked to the door. "This is the last time I'll come to visit you," he said, and left.

Cole reached out his ungloved hand and smoothed it across the bedcovers where Thomas had been sitting. He found a dozen or more traces of others there, previous occupants of the room who had come and gone, but nothing at all remained to tell him who or what his visitor had really been.

1876
Northfield, Minnesota

THE town of Northfield lay south of Minneapolis. Cole and the gang left the city on horseback, riding until they reached the wooded ground that lay to the west of Northfield. They spent that night camping with no fire lit, so as not to draw the attention of curious eyes, and when they talked, it was in low voices that wouldn't carry. The early-September air had more of a nip to it than the same air in Missouri would have, especially when the night wind blew across the tops of the pine trees with a sound like a long-drawn breath.

"Reminds me of riding in Kansas," Frank said. "Colder, though."

"Colder at Pea Ridge," Cole said, thinking of the frozen fields and the barefoot soldiers whose feet left bloody traces where they marched.

But he didn't want to turn into the kind of old soldier who talked about nothing but how much tougher everyone and everything had been back in the war; it made the newer men restive and full of beans, and liable to do stupid things just to prove that they were every bit as big and bad as everyone else. So he didn't say anything more after that. Eventually, the rest of the gang took their signal from him and fell silent as well, and from silence into sleep.

Cole, though, stayed wakeful. He spent the night turning over all the plans and possibilities in his head, when he wasn't thinking about what Thomas had said to him back in Minneapolis. *This is the last time I'll come to visit you.* The words could mean that Thomas wouldn't be coming around to bother him anymore; or they could mean that Cole wouldn't be around anymore for Thomas to bother with.

Not by steel or shot or hemp, Cole thought. *But even if he was telling the truth, that still leaves a powerful lot of ways for a man to die. Especially on a job like this.*

The next day they split up, intending to ride through town and spend the day in getting to know the lay of the land. Cole rode over the bridge that spanned yet another of Minnesota's innumerable watercourses— this one undoubtedly had a name, maybe even two or three names if the townspeople and the local Indians had proved unable to agree with one another—and into Northfield. The town was snug and prosperous, with a main street wide enough to turn a team of horses around in. The bank was a solid stone building, a regular cathedral of money with churchy-looking arched windows, big ones on the ground floor and matching smaller ones up above.

On an impulse, he stripped the glove from his right hand and laid his palm against the wall at the building's outside corner. The stone was cool to the touch, but there were no hints of possible futures in it, save for the promise that the sunlight might warm it later.

As usual, his unwanted gift wasn't useful for much besides making him uneasy and putting him off his game. Maybe the woman named Mercy could have drawn something more out of it, if she'd taken the time away from following him around through the years; or maybe Thomas could have. The both of them knew things that they weren't telling him, that was for sure.

He stepped away from the wall and strolled around the corner, marking the outside stairway that ran up the side of the bank building. The shadows lay thick beneath it—good cover—and the air smelled of horse manure and fresh blood. The former was commonplace; he wouldn't have given it a thought except that it was paired in this instance with the smell of blood, which was *not* common—or even, in this instance, real.

Dammit, he thought. *We need this to go down smooth, not bloody.*

He'd have to keep an especially keen eye on the streets outside, once the job started. To that end, he ambled north up Division Street—casual and curious, just another cattle drover in town for the day— taking note of the ways in and the ways out, the open spaces that had to be crossed on the way to safety, the places high and low where a man with a gun could take cover and do damage. He did his best not to be obvious. The war was still not so long ago that he could count on nobody recognizing the look of an old soldier scouting out the ground ahead of the action. Minnesota had turned out some damned fine fighters, as he recalled.

He walked back to the bank, went in, and got change for a silver dollar. He didn't ask any questions—folks who asked questions tended to stick in people's minds—but he glanced casually about the bank's interior, finding nothing about it out of the ordinary. Banks were like churches that way, too: so much alike on the inside, sometimes, you'd think they had rules.

Then he went back to camp and waited for the others.

One by one they arrived and drank coffee made over a small fire. While the day was still light, Cole squatted and sketched out the streets and the roads, drawing them with a twig in a patch of dirt scraped clean of pine needles, and assigned the men.

"Tomorrow," he said. "Three groups."

He pointed the twig at the youngest of his two brothers, then used it to mark an X on the scratch map. "Bob, you and Jesse and Charley Pitts are the inside men. You go into town first, you wait here in the square in front of the bank. Look casual, like you haven't got anything on your minds besides admiring the scenery, and keep in place until I give you the sign to move."

He rocked back on his heels and looked up to catch and hold their eyes. "You understand me?"

Bob nodded. "Go in first. Stay casual. Don't move until you give the word."

"We've all of us done this before," Jesse pointed out.

"But not in Minnesota," Cole said. "How about you, Charley?"

Charley spat into the dust. "Don't worry. I'm good."

"You'll need to be more than good," Cole said. "I want this job to play out with no trouble. We're not here to shoot anyone; we're not here to set fire to anything; we're here to open up the bank's safe and come away with Benjamin Butler's gold."

He marked another X on the scratch map, then pointed at Jesse's brother Frank, another old soldier, and a steady hand; then at Bill Chadwell; and last, at his own brother Jim. "I want you three in reserve here, by the bridge. That way you can block anyone who tries to follow us in, or catch up to us in a hurry if we need help. I'll want you to wreck the telegraph office, too, so the town can't organize a good pursuit—if we make off with all the bank's money, they're going to be hopping mad—but you can't do that until after the action starts."

Frank said, "You can count on us, Cap."

"Where are you going to be?" Jim asked.

"I'll be going into town last, along with Clell," Cole said. Clell Miller had ridden with them on a number of jobs, and was a good man to have around if things got rough. Cole had thought at first about putting him on the inside crew instead of Charley Pitts, but Clell had a mean streak in him when things didn't go right. He'd do better outside, where Cole could keep him level. "We'll cross the bridge and set ourselves up here and here"—he made two more X marks, one to either side of where the bank door would be—"and as soon as everyone is in place and ready, I'll give the signal. When I do, Bob and Bill and Jesse go in, shut the door behind them, get the money and the sword, and get out."

"What's so important about that sword?" his brother Bob asked him.

"It's Ben Butler's, like the money," he said. "And he'll miss it even more than he does the money, once he finds out that it's gone. When you have it, put it into my hand."

The night was another restless one for Cole, though

the others slept soundly. His thoughts kept circling back to that night before Pea Ridge, when his life had taken its first turn away from the ordinary. What would have become of him, he wondered, if General Pike and the man who called himself Mr. Thomas hadn't decided that Cole Younger was the one they needed? Everything had changed for him after that meeting, and now he could not escape the feeling that it was happening again. He hadn't known enough back then to sense the gathering of invisible forces; but he could feel them now, twisting and converging and knotting themselves together out there in the darkness among the whispering pines.

He pushed them out of his mind and concentrated on counting his own heartbeats until he fell at last into an uneasy sleep.

The gang broke camp in the morning after a breakfast of coffee and grits, rolling their blankets and strapping them to their saddles. Under the morning sun, they headed out for town.

1865

Baltimore, Maryland

KEVIN Mulcahey had never thought that he'd end his army days as a deserter. He'd been happy with his posting to the Fort Butler recruitment camp, and with the safety and the comfort of it, but he'd done his duty under fire as well and not flinched from the work. He said to himself that if it had been in a pitched battle that he'd met Captain Dykes for the second time, he would have stayed with the army and let the captain keep his sword for as long as he needed the use of it.

Instead, he found himself bent on walking across half the country with only Padraich Connor for company, all for the sake of a promise made to one of the fair folk, or to whatever Mr. Thomas might have been. The farmer's wagon and two-mule team hadn't lasted them any farther than to the next town east, where they'd put the mules, and the wagon, and the bodies of the lightning-struck bandits, into the hands of the sheriff, who would have his mind too occupied with puzzling out the wonder and the mystery of it all to spare any thoughts for a pair of sergeants passing through on army business.

"We left a pair of perfectly good horses behind in

the barn at the farmhouse," Padraich had grumbled as they left the town.

"We stole the man's cows," said Kevin. "Both of them, back in Tennessee. It's only fitting we have to travel now by shank's mare."

"Still, it's a long way to Washington, and we're not rich men, to ride there in comfort on the railroad."

"No," said Kevin. "It's deserters we are now, if we go on. But you can still take the high road back to Fort Butler, if you've a mind to, and leave the matter of the sword to me."

"I've come this far with you," said Padraich. "I'll stay with you the rest of the way."

"Are you sure?" Kevin pressed him; and Padraich said, "Aye, I'm sure"; so they began their journey east.

A hard journey it was, in the middle of winter and through a country at war. Their uniforms they soon swapped out for other garments, since to be an army sergeant is to be fair game for officers who need other men to tell the privates what to do and where to go, and after the third such mistaken impressment—with its danger of being either found out as belonging properly to the 27th Illinois, or of being swept up and sent off to join the fighting with some other regiment— they concluded that there was less risk in not wearing a uniform at all.

Winter was still a bad time to travel, though, especially for men who were trying not to be have their secrets discovered, and who had to lay over more than once when compelled by weather or by sickness or by the need to earn a bit of money to replace their dwindling store. It was spring before they reached Baltimore.

"We're almost there," Padraich said. "And we'll

have fine tales to tell our grandchildren concerning our adventures."

"If you say so," said Kevin. He had been short-tempered and grim of late, the more so as they drew nearer to the goal of their journey.

"I do say so," replied Padraich. "I'll be a happy man when our debt is discharged, and so will you. And if it will make you happier, we can afford to be spend-thrifts now, and buy ourselves train tickets to travel the rest of the way like men of leisure."

Accordingly, they took the last of the money they had in their pockets and bought themselves seats on the Baltimore and Ohio train from Baltimore to Washington. Kevin kept the sword between his knees the whole way, and clasped it in both hands as though he feared that it might vanish.

1876
Northfield, Minnesota

As soon as Cole rode into Northfield, everything started to go wrong.

He and Clell had passed by the reserve party at the bridge, holding their position as agreed, and he'd allowed himself a quick thought that it looked like the job was going to go smoothly after all. Then he checked on the inside crew loitering in the square, and they saw him doing it—his brother Bob was looking straight at him, for God's sake!—but without waiting for a word or a signal, all three of them turned and headed inside the bank.

Dammit, he thought. *I told you to wait until Clell and I had the doors!*

A shadow was following Charley Pitts, a blurring of the air, as if a part of him were lagging behind. Not the oddest thing Cole had ever seen since his life got strange, and nothing he had time to consider now. He shook his head and hurried on—what was done was done, and he'd just have to work with it. What was important now was that he and Clell had to take the bank door and close it, stop the folks outside from going in and the folks inside from going out, and keep a sharp lookout for the law.

But before they could reach the door—the door that Charley Pitts had left standing open, after Cole had told him straight out that they had to shut it behind them—a man from the town was there ahead of them, starting to go through. Clell Miller almost fell from his horse getting over there to stop the fellow. A man could get shot to death, walking in unexpectedly behind an armed man; and Cole had spent the whole ride over impressing upon the others that no one was supposed to get shot on this job.

Clell got there in time, which was good, and pulled the door shut in the citizen's face before he could go in; but the citizen stared at him wide-eyed and bolted, running around the corner past the outside stairs and yelling, "Get your guns, boys! They're robbing the bank!"

"Oh, this is good," Cole said, and swung down from his own horse. He put his back against the wall, making sure he couldn't be seen through the windows from inside the bank, and watched the street ahead. Clell was off to his right. And farther on, across Division Street, another man was shouting, "Robbery! Robbery!"

"Get the hell inside!" Cole yelled at the man. Then he glanced back at Clell, and Clell looked at him, and what Cole saw for a staggering moment was Clell dead and looking like a man who had lain on a battlefield for two days. In the next instant his sight shifted again, and he saw Clell alive; the shift made his brain whirl, as if he had sat for too long and risen too suddenly. The world turned grey and distant, like something seen at the end of a long tunnel, and he could feel it changing around him before his vision cleared and reality snapped back into place.

He fired a single pistol shot into the air, the signal for the boys on the bridge to come in and reinforce his position. As if as an echo, another pistol shot sounded from inside the bank. That meant things were either bad in there, or getting worse. And the inside crew was taking too long. They should have been in and out by now.

Cole heard the sound of hoofbeats to his left—the reserves, coming up at the gallop—and a shotgun blast to his right. He turned again in that direction and saw Clell Miller sinking to his knees, his hands clasped to his face and blood running down from between his fingers.

Dead, Cole thought. *I saw him dead before he got hit.*

"Get down, get inside!" he yelled at the people on the street. "Get away!"

He fired two more quick shots into the air. "Move!

He started toward Clell, but a bullet plowed into the dust in front of him, then kicked up into the stone wall of the bank. The man who'd first cried, "Robbery!" had gotten himself to a second-floor window across the street and was taking aim with a rifle.

Cole swung back up onto his horse. *I'll show 'em how we do it in Missouri,* he thought, and put two rounds into the window across the way.

Frank, Jim, and Bill arrived, shooting as they came. And a man stepped out into the street by the hardware store, knelt like a trooper in the line, and shot Bill Chadwell out of the saddle.

The man in the upstairs window had started aiming at their horses. First Charley Pitts's horse went down where he'd hitched it before going inside the bank, and then Bob's. Then Cole felt a burning pain, like he'd poured soup on himself, and looked down.

A bullet had torn into his thigh. He fired again at the windows across the street, to get the fellow to put his head down and to spoil his aim.

Another pistol shot sounded inside the bank. Then two more.

We're not going to get the sword or *the money,* he thought, working to reload his revolver with fingers that saw too much when they touched things. The bullet in his thigh was telling him things, too—talking about the cool customer who'd loaded a rifle, then taken aim at Cole like he was looking at an anatomy chart. *We're going to be lucky if we get out of town.*

More people were firing at them now, but mostly shooting pistols rather than long guns, and at too great a range. Cole didn't think much of their aim—but when there was enough lead in the air, aiming didn't matter so much. And that bastard with the rifle down by the hardware store was a hell of a shot.

The door of the bank opened, and Bob came pelting out. His hands were empty.

"What took you?" said Cole. He pointed to the hardware store and its defender and ordered, "Get him to put his head down!" and Bob went running off that way.

The man in the upstairs window shot at him as he passed. Bob's right arm jerked and hung limp, and blood ran down from his fingers.

"Hell with this, Cap—let's get out!" Frank yelled, at the same time winging two shots up and down the street, to remind folks that shooting at bad men was dangerous. Bullets were skipping all around.

"In the bank, let's go!" Cole shouted. "We're leaving!"

Bob climbed aboard Clell's mare that was standing

by the front of the bank. Charley Pitts and Jesse came out, the grain-sacks they'd brought along with them to carry the cash flapping loose and empty.

"Give me a hand," Cole said to Pitts. He pointed at Clell. "Boost him up on my horse, across the front, and we'll get him out of here."

One of the townspeople was down in the street, not moving. *I don't recall any of us shooting at him,* Cole thought. *Damn fool with no more sense than to run out into the middle of a gunfight. It could have been one of his own friends that did it.*

Jesse was standing over Bill Chadwell. "He's been shot through the heart!"

"Leave him," Cole said.

"Cole!" Charley Pitts said. "Help me out with Clell here!"

Charley pulled Clell Miller up and pushed him across Cole's horse, while Cole pulled on Clell's shirt from the other side. But the shirt came up and off, and Cole could see the bullet hole in Clell's chest.

The shotgun took him down, but that son of a bitch upstairs with the rifle killed him.

"He's dead too," Cole said. "Leave him. Leave them both."

"Fall back!" He raised his voice in a shout. "Fall back!"

Those others of the gang who were mounted—Frank and Jesse, and Jim and Bob—headed for the bridge. Charley Pitts's horse had been taken out by the rifleman at the upstairs window; he was still afoot.

Cole pointed to the left. "Run that way. I'll cover you."

Charley ran.

Now Cole was returning the rifle fire ball for ball,

pausing to reload, then firing again. *Get 'em to keep their heads down. Spoil their aim.* The hole in his leg hurt like thunder. Charley Pitts was twenty, thirty yards up Water Street. Cole rode after him, caught up, and pulled him up behind. Then they skedaddled.

No time now to wreck the telegraph station; the gunfire coming from behind them was getting louder, not less.

So much for the clean getaway.

"Just what the hell happened in there?" Cole asked Charley as they pounded over the bridge after the others.

"Seen a lady, said you'd told us to go in," Charley said. "Then we got in, and it all went bad."

"I was in the square and I didn't see any lady," Cole said. But then he recalled the shadow he had seen at Charley's back, and thought that he might know a lady whom it could have been.

"What happened next," Charley said, "that's my fault."

"Charley," Cole asked when the smell of whiskey hit him, Charley being so close behind, "have you been drinking?"

"Didn't think nothing of it."

"Did you kill someone, Charley?"

"He had it coming, Cole. He wouldn't open the safe."

Cole said nothing.

"He said the safe was on a time lock. Now what the hell's a time lock?"

"I should have expected it," Cole said. "The lady you talked to isn't locked in time. But all the rest of us are."

1865
Washington, District of Columbia

K EVIN Mulcahey and Padraich Connor reached
Washington on a Friday. The train pulled
in at the Baltimore and Ohio station. With a
crowd of other travelers Kevin and Padraich left their
railroad car and went out onto Massachusetts Avenue.
The street was full of carts and carriages and other ve-
hicles, as well as men and women on foot, all of them
in a hurry to get from one place to another. Kevin worried at first that the sight of a worn and dusty-looking
man—for such he knew himself to be—carrying a
sheathed sword would rouse comment, and possibly
trouble, but no one seemed to care. In the capital of a
nation at war, he reflected, perhaps such things were
commonplace.

"How do you suppose we're to find the president?"
Padraich wondered aloud. " 'Tis a busy place this is."

"He lives at the White House," said Kevin. "We can
ask for him there."

"They'll send us around to the servants' entrance,"
Padraich said. Kevin thought that he made the prediction with more relish than it deserved. "If we aren't
clapped into irons as deserters."

"That won't be necessary," said a voice nearby—

one that Kevin remembered well, for he'd last heard it on a day when bullets were whistling about his head, which is the sort of thing that concentrates the mind wonderfully. He turned, and felt no surprise to see Mr. Thomas sitting on the box of a buggy, right behind them. "Jump on, boys, and I'll take you there in style."

Kevin and Padraich looked at each other, and Kevin thought, *It's never a good idea to get into a coach with one of the fair folk*—but it was also true, as Padraich had said, that asking to see the president on their own was only likely to get them shown the door at best, or roughed up and arrested at worst. "It's your errand we've come here on," he said to Thomas after a moment's further thought. "So it's only right that you see us in."

"Then we're in agreement," said Thomas. "Good."

Kevin and Padraich got into the buggy, and they went off through the streets of Washington, down East Street to Pennsylvania Avenue and so from there to the stone wall surrounding the White House.

Their coachman must have been a known visitor— the guard at the gate waved them through without questioning them, and Thomas was able to bring the buggy up under the portico and near to the threshold without any hindrance. All three of them stepped down, and one of the White House servants mounted up into the buggy to drive it away. Kevin gripped the sword in its scabbard hard, and tried not to panic at the sight of their way out being taken away from them.

"Let's go back to Illinois," Padraich said suddenly. He sounded more afraid than Kevin had ever heard him, even at Shiloh.

They stood looking at the door. "No, let's go back to

Ireland," Kevin said. "It's Good Friday, and I haven't been to Mass in nearly four years."

"Going back to Ireland won't change that," said Thomas. "Four years lost is four years lost. Are you going to open the door or not?"

Then, "Nothing to do but do it," Kevin said. He pulled the door open, and the three of them walked in.

"The president will be up in his private rooms," Thomas said. "I know the way. Come with me."

They made their way to an upstairs parlor. A woman sat there in a chair by the window. She looked like she had been crying. When she saw the sword that Kevin carried, her eyes widened and she said, "It's the same one that I saw in my dreams—Mercy was able to find it after all."

Mr. Thomas made a noise that might have been a laugh. "It took a lot of people to find it, and to bring it here, and thanks are owing to all of them. Not that I think they'll get it."

"They'll just have to learn to go without," said another voice. Kevin saw the tall form unfolding from a chair in the shadows, and knew that it was the president himself. "It's just one thankless job among many in this life. I've been expecting something like this for a while now."

He stood and walked over to an end table covered with a white linen cloth. Then he looked at Kevin. "Lay it here," he said.

Kevin did so.

Lincoln looked over at Thomas. "This sword that Mary saw is the thing that you spoke of?"

"It is."

"And if I take it up?"

"You die tonight," Thomas said, and Kevin shuddered to hear him say it like that—not in the voice of a seer making a prediction, but as a man speaks when he states a fact already known.

"And you still don't deny that a great deal of evil will come from it?" the president asked. "Besides my death, which I have to own will be a personal inconvenience, and a grief to some."

"A great grief," said the woman, whom Kevin supposed to be the president's wife. "To many people. They will weep and wear mourning to watch you come home."

"Yes," said Thomas. "A great deal of evil, and a great deal of grief. But what happens otherwise is worse. You have the word of a sibyl on it, and mine as well—and I'm a far-traveled man. But I've come to have a powerful dislike for making other people's choices for them. In the end, the decision has to be yours."

"Four years ago," said the president, "when Fort Sumter came under fire, I took up the sword. I might as well do it now in truth."

Lincoln reached out and picked up the scabbard, then put his hand through the bell guard to hold the grip. A knock sounded on the door of the parlor, and he said, "Enter."

The door opened, and a young man came in; some sort of aide-de-camp, Kevin supposed. "Mr. President. Telegram. The flag of the Union has just been raised again over Fort Sumter."

"And Lee surrendered on Palm Sunday. I wonder what Easter will hold." Lincoln looked at the sword in his hand. "If I were to draw it," he said, "what do you think I'd find?"

"Ask Kevin there," said Thomas. "He knows."

"Red blood flowing," said Kevin, "or the sword clean. One or the other, and I don't dare guess which."

"A few days ago," Lincoln said, "I had a dream. And in it I heard sobbing. I rose, and walked through the White House. Room after room. At last, I came to a bier, laid out for a state funeral, with many people standing around it, silent. 'Who is dead?' I asked. And one of them answered, 'The president. He has been assassinated.'"

Thomas nodded, looking unsurprised. "No president has ever been assassinated yet; such are European things. But the next forty years will bring down three."

"My taking up this sword will cause this?"

"Yes."

"But you still say that it's the best way?"

"It's not a good way. But the other ways are all worse."

"I had another dream," Lincoln said. "Just last night. I dreamed I was on a phantom ship, racing toward an unknown shore. I've had that same dream three times before: before Gettysburg, before Antietam, and before Fort Fisher on Cape Fear. All great Union victories, but all accompanied by great rivers of blood. This is the same?"

And once again, Thomas said, "Yes."

God help us all, thought Kevin. *They mean for him to die, and I've brought him the reason for it.*

1876

Mankato, Minnesota

THE rest of the gang had slowed down a bit just outside of Northfield, so that Cole and Charley Pitts were able to catch up. Then they all rode on together, at a good pace but not one to kill horse-flesh—though with six men and only five horses, it wouldn't be long before the strain began to tell.

Up ahead was a farmer on horseback, heading in toward town. Cole saw Frank catch Jesse's eye and jerk his head in that direction. Jesse rode up to the farmer, pointed his .44 into the man's face, and grabbed his bridle. "Give us the borrow of your horse, friend."

The farmer had the square, resigned face of a man who didn't scare easy, but who wasn't fool enough to take on odds of one against six, either. He slid out of the saddle.

"It's yours," he said, stepping away.

Jesse raised his pistol to fire at him, but Cole shook his head. Jesse lowered the pistol, and the farmer continued his way into town on foot. Charley Pitts mounted up in the farmer's place, and the gang rode on.

That night it rained.

When they stopped, Jim Younger found that sometime in all the excitement he'd picked up a bullet in his shoulder. "Thought I'd strained it," he said.

"We'll get it seen to once we're back in Missouri," Cole said. "Right now, it can't be helped."

His own wounded leg was throbbing; he had to cut up one of the blankets with his knife to make bandages for wrapping it. Bob was in worse shape, with bone-ends visible in his elbow where the rifleman at the upper window had shot him and shattered it. They sacrificed another blanket to make him a sling, but the wound still dripped blood in slow drops.

The next day, Friday, they continued riding southwest. Everything here was trees as far as the eye could see: tall, thick-trunked white pines that stirred constantly and made whispering noises in the shifting wind. Horse tracks and deer trails came and went, skirting the edges of lakes and ponds that seemed indistinguishable one from another. The dense woods blocked the horizon and obscured the sky even when it wasn't covered by low grey clouds.

By Friday night their horses were near dead, and they were leading them. Bob and Jesse and Charley Pitts were sulky and at odds, each one blaming the others for everything that had gone wrong inside the bank. Cole privately thought that they were all to blame—Charley for bringing along the damned quart of whiskey, and the other two for not having had the backbone to turn down drinking it—but most of the fault was his own anyway, for judging it was more important to have his steadiest men waiting with the reserves.

If I'd just switched out Bill and Charley, or kept Frank and Jesse together somehow . . .

But he'd worked through the combinations over

and over inside his head, and none of them had been perfect. And none of the futures that he'd been catching glimpses of, whether he wanted to see them or not, had shown him anything that might have helped him to make a better choice. It was no wonder, he thought, that so many prophets and sibyls ultimately went mad; he was beginning to think that going mad sounded like a good idea himself.

"Maybe by now they think we're outside the county," Bob said. Walking was hard for him—every step made the bone-ends in his elbow grind together. "They could have already stopped looking for us."

"They aren't going to stop looking for us until we're out of the damned state," Cole said wearily. His leg wasn't in much better shape than Bob's elbow, even though the bone wasn't broken. He'd had to cut a stick to help himself walk. "There's a bank teller dead, and that poor stupid bastard who ran out into the crossfire. That's murder, and they'll want to hang us for it."

They walked on through the night, not stopping until the sky was streaking grey, and spent the following day on an island in the middle of a swamp, where the only sound was the whine of mosquitoes in the still air. Bob slept with his arm on Cole's chest. They left the horses there, and continued southwest on foot on Saturday night, carrying their saddles and other gear. Sunday they camped again in the woods.

On the fifth day, just as dawn was breaking, they came to a small house in a clearing. They would have passed it by, but Cole said, "Halt," and paused long enough to give the place a closer look. The house—not much more than a cabin with a porch and a brick chimney—had an overgrown and unkempt appearance, as if no one had stayed there for some months.

No smoke rose from the chimney, and there were no animals, no dogs or chickens or a horse or a cow, only the small creatures and birds of the forest.

"Charley," Cole said. "You go over and see if anyone's at home."

Cole and the others watched as Charley Pitts made his way to the cabin, taking care to stay out of sight from the windows. He went up the steps onto the porch and knocked, then gave the door a slight push. It swung open. Charley looked back over his shoulder at Cole; Cole waved a hand at him in a *move on forward* gesture. Charley entered the cabin and a few minutes later came back out again.

"It's empty," he said. "Nothing left inside but a crooked table and some wobbly-legged chairs. We can rest here for a spell."

They carried their gear into the cabin and closed the door behind them, then lay down on the floor wrapped in the remnants of their blankets. Exhaustion claimed them then, and they slept as if they were dead until the sun had reached its zenith and the air inside the cabin grew close and warm.

When Cole awoke, he saw that Frank and Jesse were already awake and watching out through the cabin window in the direction from which they had come.

"Looks like a garden out there, Cap," Frank said. "I can see watermelon from here, and beans and squash. Planted a year or so back, maybe, and gone to wild."

"Apples, too," said Jesse. "Tree's over there."

"Get a mess of them," Cole said. "And the vegetables. We could use some proper food."

Frank and Jesse went out, and Cole watched them from the window. The glass was thick and wavy, but it *was* glass, and not canvas or oiled leather. Somebody had taken pride in this place once, had put in proper windows and planted an apple tree . . . his gloves were in his saddlebags, but he had to fight down the impulse to find them and put them on. He didn't want to touch the window-frame and find out the hard way whose house this had been. A snug place like this one would have been, people didn't leave it for a happy reason.

Outside the window, Frank and Jesse were gathering up vegetables and windfall apples. The flawed glass made the yard outside the windows look blurred and strange. One moment it looked scraggy and overgrown, like it had when Cole first spotted it from the woods; then it blurred and twisted so that it made his eyes hurt, and he was looking at baked-dry ground and the skeletons of burnt-black trees. Another twist and blur, and all he saw was piles and slabs of cracked stone and rusted metal, under a yellow-hazed sky. His stomach cramped and he swallowed hard. The blurring stopped, and the world outside the window returned to normal.

The door opened again behind him and Jesse and Frank came in, bearing fruit and vegetables. Jesse cut up a melon into wedges with his knife, and Frank set to work kindling a fire and putting squash on the hearth to roast.

"Smoke'll draw the posse," Cole said.

Frank pointed to the floor where Cole had slept with Bob beside him, and where Bob and Jim still lay. Drops of blood stained the dusty floorboards. "Every step we take, you boys are leaving sign. Anyone close enough to see the smoke is following that."

Bob stirred and groaned. Jesse looked over at him,

then back at Cole. "All three of you are wounded," he said. "You're slowing us down."

Jim pushed himself to his feet, favoring his bad arm. "A day or two resting out of the wet, with a fire and food, will do us all a world of good," he said. "Speaking of which—"

"Dig in," Jesse said. He pushed a wedge of melon across the table to Jim. "Plenty more where that came from."

Charley Pitts ventured outside with their enameled tin coffeepot, and found the well. He brought back the pot full of water.

"We're out of coffee," he said. "Expect we'll get some more once we're over the border."

"How far might that be?" Jesse asked.

"Can't be over eighty miles. A week, maybe, unless we find horses."

There was silence in the cabin for a moment. Then Jesse said, "Mighty long week."

Cole gave a tired shrug. "I've seen longer."

"So what's the plan, Cap?" Frank asked.

"Missouri," Cole said. He looked hard at Frank. "We'll get there. When all this is over, you and I can sit on my front porch and talk about the good old days."

1876

Mankato, Minnesota

THE day wore on. Nobody talked much—they were all tired and bad-tempered and hurting, but so far Cole thought that no one wanted to be the first one to start a quarrel. He hoped they kept on feeling that way; penned up like this, an argument could turn nasty in a hurry.

Frank had been right about the blood trail, though. So far, Bob's wounded elbow wasn't getting worse, but it was still bleeding, and the whole left side of Jim's shirt was stiff with dried blood. And Cole's own leg throbbed whether he was walking on it or not. He sniffed at the wound. No smell of rot—that was good. Putrefaction would mean that they needed to find a sawbones, and doing that would be the same thing as putting his neck in a noose.

Along toward evening, but while it was still light out, a thin man in ragged overalls came limping up the path to the door. As soon as he reached the porch, Jesse pulled open the door, jerked the man inside, and shut the door again one-handed with a pistol jammed into the man's short ribs.

"Who sent you?" he demanded.

"No one," said the man. He had a ginger-colored

beard, and Cole thought there was something familiar about his face. "I'm just passing through looking for work."

Charley Pitts leaned pointedly against the closed door, his hand resting on his pistol grip. "Bank up to Northfield needs a new cashier," he said.

"There'll be none of that," Cole said. He regarded the man thoughtfully. "What brings you out this way, friend?"

"Looking for a roof," the man replied. "Thought it might rain, later, and the wet weather makes my game leg play up. Smelt your smoke and hoped for a place to lay my head."

"You were right about the smoke," Frank said to Cole. "Reckon I owe you an apology."

"It's all right," said Cole, still looking at the stranger. It had been a long time, but if his memory wasn't playing tricks on him . . . "You have a name, Mister—?"

"Name's Dunning," the stranger said. For a man with Jesse's pistol shoved up against his side, he seemed remarkably unperturbed. "Do you have food? I have tobacco I can share, if you need it."

"We don't have much," said Cole. "But you're welcome to some of what we have. And you," he said to Jesse, "can put up your pistol. We're among friends."

Jesse scowled but obeyed. Frank said, "You don't mind if I search him anyway, do you?"

"Go ahead. Put your mind at ease."

Frank searched Mr. Dunning quickly and efficiently, finding nothing besides the promised tobacco except some matches and rolling papers and a pearl-handled clasp knife.

"I can see he's a real dangerous sort," Bob said. He got up from his chair at the table and gestured at the remaining pieces of watermelon. "Dig in, Mr. Dunning; I've had my fill."

"When you're done," Cole said to Dunning, "I'd like a word with you in private." He looked at the others. "If he tries to kill me with his bare hands, you've got my leave to shoot him, but not otherwise."

A little while later, Cole was sitting next to Dunning on the steps of the cabin porch, his wounded leg stretched out in front of him, smoking some of that tobacco the other man had spoken of. "You're a long way from Illinois," Cole said. "And this isn't Christmas."

"You're right," said Dunning. "It isn't. But I'm a man who sees things, and I saw that one of my brothers in need of the truth would be here waiting for me. So I started walking."

"I'm in need of the truth, am I?"

"Your name was Captain Dykes the last time I saw you," said Dunning. "So you tell me."

"I saw men dead while they were still alive," Cole said. "Then I saw them die. And I don't think I'm running crazy, which just might be the first sign that I am. I don't know."

"You fought in the war," Dunning said. "Came close to dying a time or two, I'll bet."

"I might have."

"More than one man's come out of that experience with the second sight."

"I don't think that it was the war," Cole said. He gave a rueful laugh. "I think it was two old men and a fine-looking lady, and damned if I know what they were aiming at when they did it to me."

"I expect you'll figure it out in time."

"You'll have noticed that my comrades and I are

desperate men," said Cole. "I may not have enough time left to finish a job like that."

Dunning smoked for a minute in silence. Then he said, "I told you I'm a man who sees things. And I tell you, you'll have time."

"What about my friends and my brothers? What happens to them?"

"Frank'll die in bed a free man."

"And the rest of them?"

Dunning said nothing.

"It's like that, then?" said Cole.

"It's like that." Dunning pushed himself to his feet. "Let's go back inside. I've come a long way and I'm bone tired."

The next day, Cole cut himself a new walking stick from a branch of the apple tree in the cabin yard. They boiled some squash to mush, and boiled some green beans too, and ate them. The time spent resting had done the whole gang good; Jim was moving more easily, and while Bob's elbow still pained him, he had more color in his cheeks.

Late in the afternoon, with their blankets rolled and their gear packed once again into their saddlebags, Cole called Dunning over to him. "We'll be moving out soon."

"I can see that. What do you intend to do with me?"

"I've given some thought to the matter," Cole said. "Some folks"—he glanced over at Jesse, who frowned back at him—"probably think that I ought to shoot you, just to be safe. But I don't hold with violence unless it's necessary, and I think you're a man of your word."

"I try to be, yes," said Dunning.

"Good," said Cole. "So the way it goes is like this: I don't want to damn your soul. If I make you swear an oath and you break it, I'll see you in hell one day, and things will go harshly. Now you tell me, will you take your oath that you won't tell anyone else where we are until tomorrow night?"

"By tomorrow night I won't know where you've gotten to," Dunning said. "Only where you've been, and if they've got trackers with them, they'll have found that out for themselves."

"Now there's a cheerful thought," said Frank.

"But a true one," Cole said; and to Dunning, "Will you swear?"

"I'll take whatever oath you want me to."

"Swear it on your immortal soul, then, and in the name of true knowledge and the bonds of brotherhood, that you won't give away our whereabouts before tomorrow's nightfall."

"I swear it," said Dunning. Then he went back into the cabin and shut the door.

Cole and the rest of the gang walked away from the cabin and into the woods, heading north. Overhead, the last pink blush of sunset faded from the clouds, leaving only the grey behind.

Two hundred yards later, Cole stopped. "Gentlemen," he said. "Gather 'round. It's time to consider our fortunes." He stood leaning on his apple-branch walking stick and watched them as they obeyed: his brothers both like him wounded and like him slowed down by pain and weakness, and the James brothers and Charley Pitts, whom the fortunes of war had so far spared. "Frank, Jesse, Charley . . . I'd suggest that you make your way back home separately from the three of us."

"I think I'd sooner stick with you, Cole," said Charley. "If you don't mind my company."

You'll be dead either way, Cole thought. *I don't need to touch you to see it in your face.*

"I'd be honored," he said. He turned to Frank and Jesse. "The best of luck to you both, boys, and a safe journey home."

"You, too," said Jesse; but Frank stepped up and clasped Cole by the shoulders before he could duck away from the quick embrace.

"Take care of yourself, Cap," Frank said. "We'll get together again once you make it back to Missouri."

"Yes," Cole said, his voice choking a little because the touch brought with it the knowledge that Frank had, unknowing, spoken true. "We will."

But all of the others will be dead.

Then Frank and Jesse faded away under the trees. Cole stood without speaking until the woods were silent again, then pointed to the southwest.

"There's our track," he said. "I recollect we scouted out a farm down that way, near Madelia, that's got horses."

"Wouldn't the Iowa line be closer?" Charley asked.

"It might be, but they'll have been expecting us to head there straightaway, so we'll fox 'em. Besides, we need the horses."

THIS *is the strangest and most sorrowful encounter I've had yet in my life,* thought Kevin Mulcahey. *It's one thing to fight in a battle, and to know you might die in it, and another thing altogether to know that you* will *die, and with no way to fight back.*

The president took up the sword and belted it around his waist, under his dark frock coat. Kevin thought that he might have looked strange wearing it at any other time, but today the sword seemed to have found its proper place, and he didn't think that anyone seeing it would find it odd.

"Well, then," the president said, "if I'm to die tonight, I might as well have an enjoyable evening. How about the theater? A comedy would be best, I think; I'd just as soon meet my Maker with a cheerful heart."

"You know best, Mr. President," Thomas said.

The president called his aide back into the room. "Please send a message to Harry Ford that I'll be attending the performance tonight at his playhouse. Make sure the papers are all informed, for their evening edition, of where I'll be and what time I'll arrive."

Lincoln turned again to Thomas. "If it's meant to happen tonight, that should make it certain."

Thomas gave a grim chuckle. "You do know how to lead a man in the way of temptation, Mr. President."

Not for the first time, Kevin reminded himself that the fair folk were not amused by the same things as ordinary humankind—though the twist to the president's long mouth showed that he might have also smiled a little at the jest, if Mrs. Lincoln had not been sitting close by.

The president looked at Kevin and Padraich. "You did well in bringing us the sword," he said. "Now I want you to attend the theater with me tonight and see what happens." Then he turned to Mrs. Lincoln. "Would you like to come for a drive with me around the city?"

"Yes," she said. "So that I can remember how it looked on this day."

"And what of us?" Kevin said unhappily, after the president and his wife had left and he and Padraich were left alone with Thomas. "'Attend the theater,' the man says, but what else are we to do?"

"Follow his example—why not?" said Thomas. "After all the trouble you had to get here, you should take the time to see the sights. I can promise you that you won't interfere with anyone else's plans if you do so."

"What if we ask you to be our guide?" said Padraich. "For it's clear to me that you've been to this place more than once before."

"You're an observant man, Mr. Connor," said Thomas. "I'll have the buggy brought back around."

They went out into the city, and if Kevin had thought

the day was strange before, it seemed stranger now, as Mr. Thomas drove them about the city and pointed out the sights that were there to see, and sometimes the sights that were not yet there to be seen.

"Mr. Thomas," said Kevin at last, "and meaning no disrespect—*Exorcio te, creatura de forma humanis. In nomine Patre et Filii et Spiritu Sancti.*"

Thomas only laughed. "In spite of what I may have said to you once for a joke, I'm not the devil."

"It's always best to make sure," Kevin said. "How do you come to know so much, though?"

"I've lived much and seen more," Thomas said. "There are many possible worlds, and not just one world, and those who know the path can walk among them."

"Would you teach me that path?"

"No," Thomas said. "I wouldn't. I didn't choose it for myself, and what I had to do to learn it, you wouldn't like any more than I did."

"Do we live through the night?" Padraich asked.

Thomas looked at him sharply. "Why do you want to know?"

"I heard you tell the president himself that you knew that he would die. I think a man is a man, and I'm as good as him. That's what we're fighting a war about, or so I've heard tell."

"Not all questions have fixed and certain answers," Thomas said. "And a good thing, too—if the answers were fixed, there'd be no point in fighting."

They regathered at the White House at nearly seven, and after a time went to dinner. Colonel Crook, the president's bodyguard, was with them.

"Crook," the president said, "do you know I believe there are men who want to take my life? I have no doubt they will do it."

With that he sent Crook away, saying, "Go home and get some rest."

The carriage was waiting for the president and Mrs. Lincoln, with Thomas sitting inside and Kevin and Padraich standing like footmen on the rear. They paused for a while to pick up other guests, then made their way to Ford's playhouse, where the show was already in progress. The presidential box on stage left was ready and hung about with flags, and Parker, the evening bodyguard, was already waiting.

When the president and his party reached the box, Thomas turned to Kevin and said, "I want you to watch tonight. Send Parker away and take his place. A man will come. Let him in."

Kevin looked over at the president, who nodded and settled into his rocking chair. Kevin and Padraich stepped back outside of the presidential box, and stood one to either side of the door while the play progressed. About ten that night, a man with a dark mustache approached.

"Are you the man we're expecting?" Kevin asked.

"Yes."

"Then go in, your honor."

A moment passed, then another, and Kevin heard a single shot from within.

He flung open the door, Padraich at his heels, and saw Mrs. Lincoln screaming, and the president sitting in his rocker, his eyes closed and blood running on his shoulder, and the dark-haired man leaping over the balcony railing. Padraich reached out to grab him, but only took his spur in his hand, for that was as far as he could reach. The spur came free, and the man completed his leap to the stage.

"*Sic semper tyrannis!*" came the shout from below, but Kevin paid it no heed.

Thomas was there in the box with them, holding the sword. "The president has been shot," he said. "Go, and take this with you."

"What should I do with it?"

"You'll know what's best when the time comes. Now go, before the police arrive and everything is chaos."

1876
Madelia, Minnesota

Two weeks after Northfield, on a Thursday, Cole and his brothers and Charley Pitts were nearing Madelia. They'd had some close calls, but fewer and fewer of them as time went on, and their injuries were starting to heal. None of their wounds were swelling up, smelling foul, or dripping pus, and the blood-trail was no longer marking where they had been.

"I'm starting to think we might get back to Missouri after all," Bob said. "We haven't gotten so much as a whiff of pursuit for three days now."

"Nothing's certain," said Cole. The voices of the cards he'd touched back during the poker game in Minneapolis whispered again in his ears: *Last game. Never again.* He'd pulled his gloves out of his saddlebags days ago, and wore them in spite of the September heat, lest he accidentally touch one or another of his companions and learn yet one more secret that he didn't want to keep. "But every step we take gets us that much closer."

"River up ahead," his brother Jim observed. "Looks too deep for wading."

"And we're most of us too banged up to swim it," Bob said. "Except for Charley, here."

"Damned if I'm going to be the only one getting wet," Charley said. "I say we find a bridge and go across it."

"Tonight, then," said Cole. "After dark."

Then we get to Madelia, he thought, *and steal some horses. We have to keep on trying, because nothing is fixed for certain. Elsewise, Thomas and Mercy wouldn't be taking it in turns to push me where they think I should go.*

"I am tired of skulking around in the dark," Charley said. "Yonder's the road. I'm following it."

"Damn fool's going to get us all killed," Bob said, but he followed Charley, and Jim did likewise.

"Might as well stick together," Cole said, and went after them. They crossed the river bridge when the road came to it, and despite Cole's misgivings they saw no one along the way. They were out of the deep woods now, and into farmland dotted with trees and brush, and more of the inevitable lakes and ponds and small watercourses.

"The farm with the horses is in that direction," he said, pointing. He'd been there before—it felt like forever ago now—while he was scouting out the area before the raid, the way that he'd learned while riding with Quantrill, making sure there was a way in and a way out. "Through the trees."

They were just coming around toward the farm, making their way through the stand of trees and brush beside the river, when they heard horses on the road behind them: men riding slowly. A whole troop of them.

Charley Pitts cursed. Bob groaned. Jim looked at Cole with a question in his eyes.

"Nothing for it but to go on," Cole said.

They came out of the trees, and ahead of them

stood a line, dressed and covered, forty men if there was one, holding pistols and long guns. There was nothing behind Cole and the gang but an unfordable river, and nothing ahead but the paddock with the fresh mounts, in sight but out of reach.

"Back!" Cole shouted, and went for the brush. "We can wait 'em out. Come dark we'll come by 'em."

"Not going to work, Cole," Jim said. "They're coming in after us." And so it was: ten of the forty were advancing in line at the double-quick, and firing pistols into the heaviest brush as they came.

"Charley," Cole said. "You can surrender. I won't think any less of you."

"To hell with that," Charley said. "I can die as well as you can."

"Better to live, if you get the chance," Cole said. "On my signal, head for the horses. Every man for himself. Stand by—*now*!"

A fusillade. Smoke. Another crash of gunfire, and Cole fell into blackness shot through with red pain, radiating from the center of his chest.

1876

Madelia, Minnesota

C OLE had taken wounds before, riding with
Quantrill and with the Missouri militia in the
war, but never so many as he had when the
posse at Madelia brought him down. Some of the bullets were in him still; the doctor that the sheriff had
brought in to take care of him and his brothers said
that those were the ones it would be more dangerous
to take out than to leave alone. Cole thought that it
was mighty kind of the State of Minnesota to be so
tender of a bunch of men they were almost certainly
planning to hang—it wasn't like there was going to
be any shortage of witnesses at the trial, and he didn't
think the jury would believe him if he claimed it was
all a tragic misunderstanding—but he was coming
around to the opinion that Minnesotans, all things
considered, were a decent sort of people.

The sheriff in charge of the posse could have shoved
his wounded prisoners into a jail cell, but instead had
chosen to put them up in the Flanders House Hotel in
Madelia, under guard. If Cole had had the strength
for it, he might have laughed, or maybe wept—he and
Charley Pitts had stayed for a night in the same hotel
when they were scouting out the land before the raid.

But Charley was dead now, shot through the heart in that last furious exchange of gunfire.

Cole himself, the doctor said, not being dead yet, was reckoned likely to live in spite of all the lead in him. His brothers were in worse case, Bob shot through the lung and Jim with bullets lodged in his upper jaw and in his spine. But they weren't dead yet either, and would probably last at least long enough to be tried.

After the doctor left, while Cole was lying hand-cuffed to the hotel bed and contemplating the pattern in the wallpaper, another visitor came to see him. He didn't ask how she had come all the way to Minnesota, or from where, or how she had made her way, a woman alone, past all the guards outside—he knew by now that Mercy had her own gifts, and her own ways of travel.

She sat down in the straight-backed chair by his bedside and said, "Hello, Mr. Younger."

"Have you come here to weep over me?" he asked. She was wearing black today, gown and hat and a black crepe veil; not full widow's weeds, but funeral dress for someone she knew well.

"No," she said. "I've come here to thank you."

"For what? We never even got into the damned safe, and that sword you said I was supposed to fetch is still in there."

She looked down at her hands; she was wearing black lace mitts, and her fingers were twined hard together. "This is the part that isn't easy for me to say. But it isn't right that you should be left ignorant, either."

"Ma'am," he said, with what he thought was a fair amount of patience under the circumstances, "I've got eleven bullet wounds in me and all of them hurt; also, the state of Minnesota wants to hang me by the neck until I'm dead. Whatever you've got to say to me can't make things much worse."

"The sword was never in the bank vault at all."

Cole looked at the wallpaper some more, until he could trust himself to speak. "You sent me here on purpose, knowing that."

"Yes," she said. "Knowing that you would fail, and that you would be taken."

"Why?"

"Because if you plead guilty, Minnesota won't hang you. The state saves the expense of a trial, and you go to prison."

"Prison," he said. "For how long?"

"For life."

He looked at her hands, still twisted hard together. "That was the whole point. Of everything. To get me locked up for the rest of my life."

"Yes," she said, low voiced.

"Why?"

"Because you were promised the time and the quiet that you needed, and this is the way you get it."

"*Thomas*, god damn him." Cole shut his eyes, once again not knowing whether to laugh or to weep.

"Oh, Mr. Younger." Mercy's voice trembled, as if she also could not choose between mirth and tears. "Haven't you figured it out?"

"Figured what out?"

"Thomas Coleman Younger. You *are* Mr. Thomas."

"Damnation," he said. Then, "I can't say it changes my opinion of him any."

"Nevertheless, I owe him my thanks, for helping me to keep a promise to a friend. And I owe you an apology, for helping him make you become him."

"I'll let you know when I figure out which end of that apology is which."

"Ouroboros," she said. "The serpent of eternity, that bites its own tail forever."

"That was a good afternoon," he said. "That time in Florida."

"Yes," she said. "It was."

"You can be sorry for anything else you like—I'm still not happy about being set up and shot at and slapped into prison—but don't be sorry about that. If you're right about the State of Minnesota, then I expect to be remembering that day fondly for a good long time."

"That's very . . . kind . . . of you to say so," she said, and he saw the color rise briefly in her cheeks. Then her expression changed back to its former gravity, and she rose from her chair. "I have to leave you now; I've stolen the time for this visit from those who will miss me if I'm away for much longer. Good-bye, Mr. Younger."

"Good-bye," he said, and watched her black taffeta skirt sway around her ankles as she crossed the room. "Mercy?"

She halted with her fingers touching the doorknob. "Yes, Mr. Younger?"

"Am I ever going to see you again?"

"Yes," she said. "Once more. But not for a very long time. Meanwhile"—she paused, seemed to recall something, and smiled at him—"exercise patience. And restraint."

With that, she opened the door and passed through it, and out of his sight.

1865

Washington, District of Columbia

K EVIN Mulcahey stood on the bank of the Potomac River and listened to the sounds of the city behind him. As Thomas had foretold, chaos had come. Soldiers and policemen were searching everywhere for the vanished assassin, and rumors were rife. Shouts and alarum bells had punctuated the darkest hours of the night and even now had not entirely faded.

"I'd not like to be that villain when they catch him," said Padraich, low voiced. It had not been a night for a pair of deserters to say anything that might draw the attention of those who wouldn't understand their reasons for departing the army without official leave. "Nor one of his friends, either."

"Nor I," said Kevin. "You said we'd have a tale to tell our grandchildren, but I'm thinking that we won't be able to tell this tale to anyone at all."

"Will you be keeping that, then?" Padraich asked him, with a nod of his head at the sword in its scabbard.

"To hang over my fireplace and remember the war?" Kevin said. "I don't think I'll be needing it for that."

"No," agreed Padraich. "Neither will I."

"Thomas said that I'd know what to do with it."

"That's no great wisdom. Once you make up your own mind, you'll know it."

"So I'm supposed to choose." Kevin weighed the weapon across his two hands, blade and belt and scabbard. "It's a fine sword, I've no doubt, even if it's a strange one. If I could find the rebel I took it from, back at Belmont, I'd give it to him again, but he's dead. Or if I thought that I could do it without having every soldier and policeman in Washington leap onto me at once, I'd leave it on Mr. Lincoln's bier."

"As well think of giving it back to Captain Dykes."

"Another strange fellow," said Kevin. "But he's gone who knows where, and there's no one left with a proper claim."

"Then sell it to Mr. Barnum, if you want money, or give it to a historical society, if you don't. Only be careful. Remember what happened to the last people who tried to keep it when they had no right."

"I remember," said Kevin.

Abruptly, he straightened, and lifted his head from contemplation of the blade. Then he took it scabbard and all into his right hand, and flung it out into the deep part of the river, where it hit the water with a loud splash.

"There," he said. "Now no one has it, and all have it."

And the ripples spread outward as the sun rose over the city.

Authors' Note

THIS story is, of course, a work of fiction, and fantastical fiction at that; any characters appearing in it are not in any way to be considered as representative of their historical counterparts. Mary Todd Lincoln was certainly not a prophetess, and her friend Mercy Levering Conkling was not a mystical adept; and Cole Younger, while he was most certainly a Civil War guerrilla fighter and later a member (and quite probably the actual leader) of the notorious James-Younger gang, was likewise not a practitioner of any magical arts. He was, however, by all accounts an engaging and likable man, spoken well of even by his enemies, and his memoirs, *The Story of Cole Younger, by Himself; Being an Autobiography of the Missouri Guerrilla Captain and Outlaw, his Capture and Prison Life, and the Only Authentic Account of the Northfield Raid Ever Published*, make interesting reading.

General Albert Pike, on the other hand, really was almost as strange in real life as his fantastical counterpart in this novel. After the Civil War, he became one of the primary movers in the establishment of Scottish Rite Freemasonry in America, and wrote extensively on esoteric Masonic subjects. He was admired enough by his fellow-Masons to have a statue erected in his honor in Washington, D.C.; his detractors, on the other hand, have over the years accused him of being, among other things and at various times, a Satanist, a Ku Klux Klansman, and a member of the Bavarian Illuminati. He remains, unsurprisingly, a figure of controversy.

LEGENDS OF THE RIFTWAR

HONORED ENEMY
978-0-06-079284-8

by Raymond E. Feist & William R. Forstchen

In the frozen northlands of the embattled realm of Midkemia, Dennis Hartraft's Marauders must band together with their bitter enemy, the Tsurani, to battle *moredhel*, a migrating horde of deadly dark elves.

MURDER IN LAMUT
978-0-06-079291-6

by Raymond E. Feist & Joel Rosenberg

For twenty years the mercenaries Durine, Kethol, and Pirojil have fought other people's battles, defeating numerous deadly enemies. Now the Three Swords find themselves trapped by a winter's storm inside a castle teeming with ambitious, plotting lords and ladies, and it falls on the mercenaries to solve a series of cold-blooded murders.

JIMMY THE HAND
978-0-06-079299-2

by Raymond E. Feist & S.M. Stirling

Forced to flee the only home he's ever known, Jimmy the Hand, boy thief of Krondor finds himself among the rural villagers of Land's End. But Land's End is home to a dark, dangerous presence even the local smugglers don't recognize. And suddenly Jimmy's youthful bravado is leading him into the maw of chaos . . . and, quite possibly, his doom.